The Last Good Seat at the Bar

Emily Coleman

Trade Street Press

TRADE STREET
PRESS

Printed in the United States of America

ISBNs:
Paperback: 979-8-218-73922-5
Hardcover: 979-8-9931964-0-4
eBook: 979-8-9931964-1-1

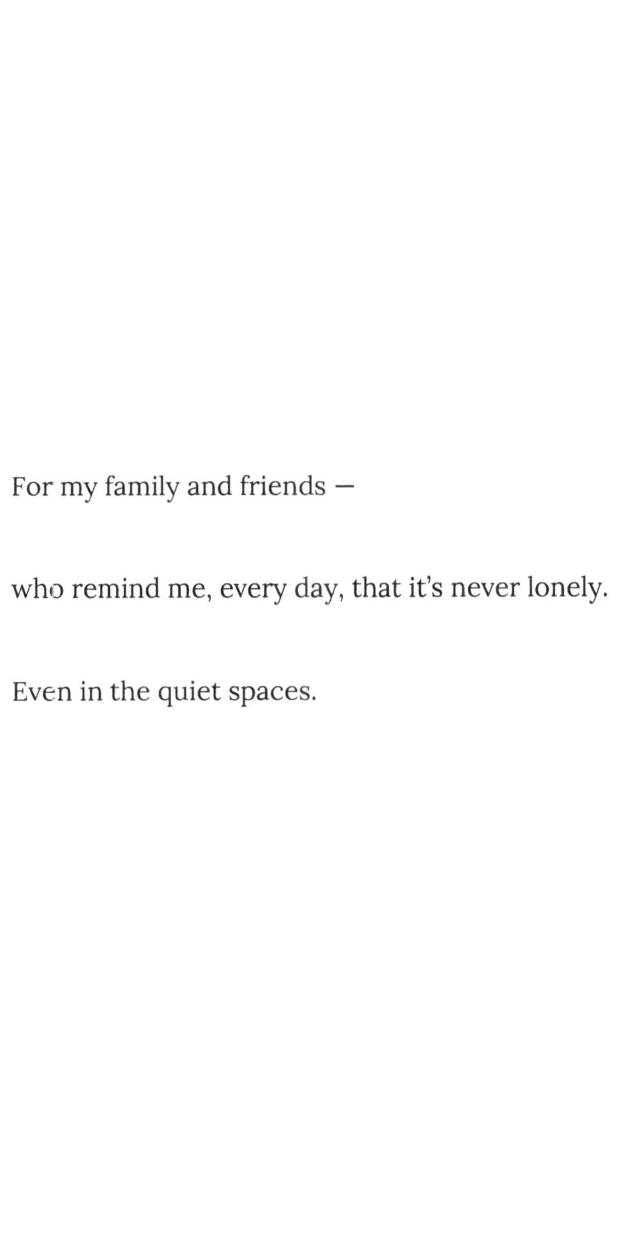

For my family and friends —

who remind me, every day, that it's never lonely.

Even in the quiet spaces.

I'm just trying to find something real in all the noise.

— Bruce Springsteen,
Springsteen: Deliver Me From Nowhere (2025 film)

CHAPTER 1

I was empty and full of light

Morgan Langford sat on the edge of her couch, elbows on her knees, staring into the quiet. The apartment felt thinner than usual these days, like a tent with one side unzipped.

There was a history documentary about the Founding Fathers on television, but she had turned the volume down. The remote slipped between the couch cushions, half buried beneath her knee. She didn't bother retrieving it. The images were familiar, almost comforting, but at the end of the day, there were only so many documentaries that offered new and exciting Founding Father facts.

The pile of laundry folded neatly on the coffee table, the nearly empty bourbon bottle on the counter — both things she kept meaning to do something about. She hadn't. Not yet. She tried not to look at it too long.

Her eyes were open but not focused. The apartment wasn't dirty. Just... cluttered. Surfaces hadn't been wiped down in a while, but they weren't sticky. The carpet near the couch showed the vague outline of where she'd paced barefoot. A pair of boots sat by the door, one tipped over, waiting for a reason to be worn. Books were stacked on the floor near the radiator — some she'd finished, some she hadn't, all of them holding her place in a way she couldn't do right now. Life looked paused.

She stood and crossed to the kitchen. Not to cook — she hadn't done that in weeks — but to find the water bottle she'd half-drained last night and never capped. She drank from it anyway, swallowing the flat taste of yesterday's tap.

On the table, her laptop sat closed, probably completely dead. She ran her finger across the top and wiped away the lightest trace of dust. It was the first time she'd touched it in days. She didn't open it.

Her phone buzzed on the counter. She picked it up, thumbed past unread texts, and tapped on the most recent voicemail.

"Morgan I didn't want to do this over voicemail, but I haven't been able to reach you by phone. I spoke to Katherine and we think it's best you take some time— call it a sabbatical, call it whatever makes sense. Just... step away for a while."

Her editor's voice paused, hesitant, like he'd reached the end of his usefulness and didn't know how to land the plane. Then the line clicked off.

Morgan let the silence hang. It wasn't a shock. She hadn't turned in a clean piece in weeks. The writing wasn't blocked anymore — it just wasn't there. Nothing stirred.

She set the phone down gently. No anger. No surprise.

Elise had left six weeks ago. Morgan leaned back into the couch, spine catching awkwardly against the frame. Her eyes drifted to the spot on the bookshelf where Elise's books used to be. She missed the way her classical guitar filled the apartment and echoed off of every wall. She could make your heart ache and put a smile on your face at the same time. In the end it was one suitcase, one goodbye. It hadn't been cruel, just finished. None of it was Elise's fault. They both knew that.

She pulled a chair out from the table and sat, staring out the window. The morning sun caught the empty bottle above the cabinet. Only one — she didn't let it get that far — but she'd started moving them to the recycling bin one at a time. Like she could outpace her own noticing.

The next few days blurred into an out-of-tune symphony of sleeping, bourbon, old television shows, online orders left outside the apartment door. Bourbon. More bourbon.

On the third night, she stood up too fast, her legs unsteady and tripped over the corner of the rug. Her temple caught the edge of the coffee table before she collapsed onto the carpet. The room spun as she pressed her hand against her face, waiting for the sting to pass. When she finally looked in the mirror, a bruise had already started to bloom, purpling at the edge of her eye. She laughed once — a hollow, humorless sound — and poured another drink.

The bruise deepened the next morning, a spreading shadow she tried not to see when she caught herself in the bathroom mirror. She dabbed at it with cold water, pulled her hair forward, and left it at that.

Late that afternoon, her friend Claire let herself in with the spare key. "Morgan?" Her voice carried that mix of cheer and suspicion she used when she knew something wasn't right. She stepped into the living room and froze.

Morgan was on the couch, wrapped in a quilt, the bourbon bottle half-drained on the table. The bruise was plain, even in the half-light of the room.

"Jesus, Mor," Claire said, setting her bag down. She crouched in front of her, tilting her chin gently to look at the eye. "What the hell happened?"

"I tripped" Morgan muttered, pulling back. "It's nothing."

"Nothing? You look like you went three rounds with a brick wall." Claire's voice was sharp, but underneath it was fear. "You've been dodging my texts. You look like—" She stopped herself. "You can't stay like this."

Morgan tried to laugh, but it came out cracked. "I'm fine."

"No, you're not." Claire's eyes flicked to the bourbon bottle, then back to her. "I'm not here to lecture you, but you've got to do something before this place eats you alive." She reached for Morgan's phone on the table. "Call Margaret."

"Don't."

"Then I'll do it." Claire held the phone out. "She'll come up here herself if she has to, and you know she will."

Morgan stared at the phone, her jaw tight. The weight of the silence pressed until she finally reached out and took it. She didn't dial, not yet, but she held it in her lap, thumb brushing the screen like it might burn.

"I can't..."

"Yes, you can." Claire sat beside her, looping an arm around her shoulder. "One call. Just tell her what's going on. You don't have to figure everything out right now. Just... don't keep sinking. This is worse than last time."

Morgan swallowed hard, the words sticking. She could smell Claire's shampoo, clean and sharp against the stale air of the apartment. Her chest tightened until the only thing left to do was breathe through it.

"Remind me to take your key away from you," Morgan said softly.

Claire smiled, but it was thin. "Just promise me you'll call her."

Morgan didn't promise. But that night, when she picked up her phone again, she scrolled through the contacts until she found Margaret's number.

Friday around 11 a.m., before she could talk herself out of it, she pressed call.

Two rings.

"Morgan?" Margaret's voice arrived warm and measured, with a careful kind of concern.

"Hey."

"Oh, honey. I'm glad you called." No pressure. No lecture.

"I think I got fired? Or something like it. They said sabbatical. That's just a gentler way of saying please disappear."

"I'm so sorry," Margaret said quietly. "What can I do to help? Do you need me to come up? Do you need help with money at all?"

"No, no Margaret. I don't want you to drive all this way. It's too much for you and money's fine. I have enough in savings. I just wanted you to know and hear your voice."

Margaret sat quiet for a beat and said softly, "I've been meaning to talk to you about something. You know the old cabin's been empty for some time now."

"The Bar?"

"Yeah... Dad's old place. It's a little rough. Needs a deep clean, but it's solid. The front steps are holding—barely—but the rest is good. There are a few quiet neighbors, but mostly trees and marsh, and space for you to breathe. Sometimes that can make more difference than you realize."

Morgan hesitated. Her memories of the place were flashes: porch steps under her five-year-old feet, the smell of fishing, cricket baskets and Lucky Strike cigarettes. Cousins and other relatives coming and going, the steady beat of music bleeding through knotty pine walls. Granddad's voice telling her to keep the wheel steady as she sat on his lap, the truck rattling down the dirt road. He had decided to leave this world not long before her tenth birthday, and after that the cabin had become more of a myth in her mind than an actual memory.

Margaret's voice softened. "You clean it up, fix what's needed, and stay as long as you like. I think it might do you both good." She paused. "It seems a shame to let something so loved continue to be empty. After your uncles moved away, nobody seemed to have the time for it."

Morgan looked around the apartment. The bourbon bottle. The untouched planner. The windows closed against a city she no longer felt part of.

"Okay," she said quietly. "Yeah... I'll go. Thank you, Aunt Margaret."

Margaret didn't hide her relief. "Good. I'll text you the code for the lock box. Drive safe, honey, and let me know when you get there. And Morgan?"

"Yes, ma'am?"

"I love you."

"I love you too."

She left two days later, just after noon. It was March and, even though the sky was cloudless and the sun was bright, she could still see her breath.

She didn't pack much. An oversized duffel with jeans, t-shirts, sweatshirts, notebooks she hadn't touched in months. A cooler with apples, hard cheese, and bottled water. She didn't say goodbye to anyone except Claire, who gave her a long look and squeezed her shoulder at the door.

The roads out of Atlanta blurred quickly — glass and steel giving way to pine trees and peeling paint. Billboards turned into tree lines. Suburbs became long stretches of Low Country, flat and shimmering. The drive didn't feel like an escape. It felt like drifting through time. Backwards and slow.

The radio was down but Morgan turned it up when she heard a familiar song. Billy Joel. "Just The Way You Are".

Years ago, she and her friend Ashley had driven this same stretch after coming back from a concert — windows down, barefoot, the marsh a blur. Morgan hadn't thought of that night in a long time. But now, with the sun slanting through the windshield and the sky that soft Carolina blue, it came back whole.

Ashley had been singing along. Morgan had watched her the whole time — just watched her — and realized the ache she had felt for so many years wasn't going to go away. She would have to be the one to leave. Once the song ended, Morgan turned the radio off completely and with it the memory.

By early evening, she was in South Carolina. Morgan made a mental note at the first produce stand. Fresh peaches and boiled peanuts. Still early in the season, but it wouldn't be too long. She could definitely find some of those close to home. The air had changed. It was thicker, richer. It carried the scent of earth and salt and days upon days upon days.

She followed the GPS until the screen turned blank. Then came the long dirt road, nearly swallowed by trees and vines. The mailbox was crooked now. The sign above the porch still read BILL'S BAR — hand-painted, cracked from sun and years of weather. Not a real bar, of course. Just the nickname that had stuck. If any of Granddad's buddies from town said they were headed to The Bar, their wives knew they would be with Granddad at their favorite spot. The running joke was no matter how many people showed up, the person walking through the door at the time was getting the last good seat.

In other words, there was always room for one more.

Now, Morgan parked at the edge of the clearing and stepped out into the late light. The front sagged slightly, porch leaning like a tired man. The screen door rattled in the breeze. Spanish moss dangled from low branches like old lace.

Margaret had exaggerated a bit about the state of the place. Morgan had a feeling that would be the case. There was a property manager who kept the grounds in order, maintained the plumbing and HVAC, and made sure the roof wasn't actually falling in. Also, conveniently, there was a stack of freshly split firewood on the side of the porch. Thank you, Aunt Margaret.

There were still enough small tasks that would make Morgan feel like she was needed here.

She climbed the sagging porch steps, took the key from the lockbox, and pushed.

Inside, the air felt a bit stale and thick. Furniture stood in ghostly outlines beneath old sheets. Dust shimmered in the final sunbeams of the day. The stone fireplace sat cold and empty, and Granddad's vintage Magnavox HiFi console on the far wall looked untouched. It was one of the first systems with a multi-record changer and instead of a volume knob it read "Loudness." That memory made Morgan smile.

She stood just inside the doorway for a while, taking it in. Nothing stirred.

She pulled the sheet from the couch, shook it outside, then returned to brush off the cushions with her hand. They were firm. Sturdy enough. She found an old patchwork quilt and a pillow folded in the cedar chest behind the couch. She'd sleep there tonight.

She didn't clean much else. Her body was already settling. Everything else could wait. She needed only the couch and a place to breathe.

She opened a couple of windows long enough to air the cabin. A cold breeze carried in the smell of the marsh. Sharp and honest.

She flipped through the albums on the shelf and found Sinatra. She placed several discs on the changer, pressed play, and let the sound fill the hollow.

Morgan curled up on the couch beneath the quilt and let herself be still.

The cabin didn't welcome her. It didn't reject her either. It simply waited.

Like it knew it would see her again.

CHAPTER 2

Gradually, then suddenly

Morgan woke to filtered light and the sound of wind moving softly through the trees behind the cabin. The quilt she'd pulled over herself had twisted around her legs, and she could feel the sharp angle of the couch's center cushion pressing into her ribs.

She stretched one arm overhead and let her eyes adjust to the room. It didn't look much better in the daylight—still dusty, corners threaded with web—but it felt quiet. Like the house was doing its best not to wake a rare guest. The room felt like it was holding its breath in the way just before someone speaks.

Morgan sat up slowly and walked sock-footed into the kitchen. The air inside was dense with the scent of old wood and the kind of missed cleanings that add up over time. That could wait for now. She merely opened a few drawers, tapped the thermostat up a notch to take the chill off and listened to the pipes. The water sputtered and ran a translucent khaki for a moment, then cleared. Small blessings.

She boiled water in the old kettle and steeped some tea she'd brought from Atlanta. As it brewed, she sat on the floor with her back against the cabinets and watched the dust drift in the light. No one knew she was here except Aunt Margaret and Claire. For now, that was exactly how she wanted it.

She didn't think she'd miss the city. Or the apartment. Or the grind of routine. What she missed— what hollowed her out—was the writing. Not the deadlines or the meetings. Just the act of writing. The part where the words flowed faster than she could catch them. That feeling had been gone for months now. Burnout, she had told herself. Just stress. A creative lull. But she knew better. It wasn't stress. It was silence.

And when the silence took hold, it brought everything else with it: the doubt, the drinking, the gradual unraveling of things she thought were solid.

More than one relationship had folded in on itself during these times, not with fireworks, but with quiet fatigue. She didn't blame anyone for that. It was inevitable. When the words stopped, she stopped. And it turns out, that was harder to be around than most people could imagine.

Here, though, the silence didn't feel cruel. Just present. Like weather. And yet underneath it was something sharper—an edge. The thought of being back at The Bar unsettled her in ways she hadn't admitted to Margaret on the phone. This place wasn't just a cabin. It was where her Granddad had lived his last days, where his absence had first taken root. Coming back meant walking into rooms that still carried the echo of that loss. Part of her feared the house remembered him better than she did.

Morgan threw on a warm hoodie, grabbed her keys from the wooden bowl beside the porch door and made her way back down the winding drive. She knew exactly where she was headed. Truluck's. Part grocery store, part farmers market, part bait and tackle. It was also close to home, and she wouldn't have to go all the way into town. Just a few staples and some cleaning supplies.

When Morgan returned, the house felt like it was holding its breath again—waiting to see if she'd stay. If she'd continue.

She did.

Back in the living room, Morgan flipped through Granddad's records and found a compilation with Coltrane's "In a Sentimental Mood" on it. She set it on the turntable, dropped the needle, and let the gentle piano ripple across the space. The saxophone followed—smooth, slow, almost conversational.

She moved to the bookcase beside the fireplace. The shelves were dusty and uneven. Some books were stacked horizontally, others jammed in at odd angles. Most were dog-eared paperbacks—fishing guides, almanacs, a few gardening manuals that looked untouched. But on the middle shelf, she found the familiar spines.

There he was. Hemingway. A full row of him. Granddad's worn copies of *The Sun Also Rises*, *A Farewell to Arms*, *For Whom The Bell Tolls*. A collection of his short stories, the cover curling slightly at the edges. Even a thick volume of letters, the kind nobody really reads cover to cover.

She crouched down in front of them and ran her fingers across the spines. Her granddad, like many others, had called him Papa. Not Hemingway—Papa. Like they'd known each other. Like he was family. He used to talk about him with reverence, though Morgan had been too young to understand it then. She remembered the way he'd say, "That man knew how to write clean," or "Papa didn't waste time on nonsense," usually while tapping the book for emphasis with his index finger. It takes special talent to write like that and still write big. That's how Granddad referred to someone who wrote novels—writing BIG.

Morgan had grown up with those stories. If Granddad had a hero in this life, Papa was that hero. He mentioned trying to write some when he was a younger man, but he must not have kept any of it. Or perhaps it was one of those things people say they did, like being in a band. As a teenager, Morgan started reading Hemingway for herself, mostly out of curiosity, partly to feel attached to Granddad. Then all at once, she understood.

There was something spare in the prose that left room for the reader to breathe. It wasn't sentimental. It wasn't trying to be clever. It just was. Like the sea. Or the marsh.

She wondered now if that was part of what scared her. If she let herself sit too long in this house, surrounded by his books and his voice in her memory, she might have to face the fact that he had left her here—not just by dying, but by dying the way he did. Coming back to The Bar meant walking a line between reverence and resentment.

Years ago, during a spring trip to Key West, she'd gone to Hemingway's home. The tour had moved slowly through the rooms, each one held together by sunlight and humidity. She hadn't taken pictures. She'd barely listened to the guide. She just stood there in the doorway of the upstairs study, looking at the old Royal typewriter and the worn floors beneath it. It had reminded her of The Bar. The stillness. The heat. The way the walls seemed to lean slightly inward, like they were straining to hear what you were thinking.

She reached out now and pulled down the short story collection. The cover cracked softly in her hands. She settled into a wicker chair with the book in one hand and a cold beer in the other. She noticed the way the beer sat easy in her hand—different from the bourbon, which always seemed heavier. She didn't dwell on it. A passing thought.

She read until the light changed. By late afternoon, shadows from the trees stretched long across the walls. The air inside the house had cooled down, and the sounds outside had shifted—fewer birds. The marsh had many instruments and, as it became warmer, the symphony would grow and change.

Morgan stood and stretched. She returned the book to the shelf, paused for a second, then let it go. The records had stopped.

She put on Loretta Lynn. She let the needle fall and Loretta's voice trailed out across the floor. It filled the room differently than Coltrane had. Coltrane had drifted. Loretta settled in like a broken heart that would linger.

Morgan lit a candle she'd found in the kitchen drawer and set it on the windowsill. The flame flickered gently against the glass. She didn't feel peaceful, but she felt still, and that was enough for now.

She made a light dinner. The night wrapped around the cabin, not heavy, just certain. She checked the doors, turned off the kitchen light, and settled back onto the couch beneath the quilt.

The records kept playing quietly in the corner. As she lay there, eyes adjusting to the dark, she thought again of the books on the shelf and her grandfather, sitting in this same room thirty years ago, bourbon in hand, saying something about Papa making a sentence bleed.

She thought of Key West. The quiet of it. The way the floorboards had creaked. She thought—just briefly— about what it would take to write again. Not today. Maybe not tomorrow. But eventually. Maybe here.

The rocking chair by the fireplace gave a quiet creak. Morgan opened one eye. Stared at it for a long moment. No breeze, no movement. Just the creak. Then stillness.

She didn't sit up. She didn't move at all. She let the sound exist without needing to explain it.

And when the records stopped, she let the HiFi shut itself down. She closed her eyes, let her hand rest against her chest, and listened to the silence that followed.

It didn't feel like only a memory anymore. It felt like a beginning.

CHAPTER 3

Strong at the broken places

The day started, theoretically, before sunrise. Not suddenly, but gradually — the way light weaves in around the side of a curtain and softens the edges of sleep until the day becomes undeniable.

She lay still for a minute, listening. No traffic. No city hum. Just the old groan of the house settling and the faint rustle of leaves outside. The couch left a dull line across her cheek. The quilt had slipped off sometime in the night, and her feet were cold.

She sat up slowly and looked around the room. Something in her had shifted — not dramatically, but enough to notice. Her body didn't feel as heavy this morning. Her thoughts didn't arrive with the usual static.

She was still tired, but not in that dull, marrow-deep way she'd grown used to. This was a natural tired. The kind that came from being in motion. And that, she thought, was a kind of progress.

She stood and stretched her arms overhead, spine giving a muted crack as she twisted side to side. The couch groaned beneath her as she stepped away and she pulled the quilt around her shoulders like a cape.

In the kitchen she could see the early light filtered through the screen door and settled in pale slats across the porch floor. The air smelled faintly cleaner than yesterday — citrus and something a little sharper, like old pine warming in the sun.

She filled the kettle and set it on the burner. The stove ticked as it warmed, and she leaned against the counter with both hands flat, watching the thin trail of steam start to rise.

Morgan carried the mug into the living room and sat in the rocker by the window, letting the floorboards settle beneath her. The tea was hot enough to slow her down, which was what she liked about it. It gave her something to do while doing nothing.

The trees were still this morning. No birdsong yet. Just that low, constant breath from the marsh that never fully stopped. It wasn't silence — more like a resting pulse.

Morgan had always been good at being alone. Not in a wounded way, and not out of pride. It was just how she came up.

She'd lost her parents before she had language for what losing meant. A two-year-old's memories stick in the form of trauma, not detail. A car crash, some late-night highway in South Georgia, and everything she should have remembered dissolved before it could root.

Aunt Margaret had taken her, raised her with a soft touch and steady hands. Granddad had been the bigger presence — louder, gruffer, the kind of man whose affection came in acts, not words. He'd taught her how to bait a hook, how to use the record player without letting the needle scratch, how to oil a hinge to keep it from squeaking. He didn't talk about grief, but he knew how to sit beside it without blinking.

By the time Morgan was eleven, she'd stopped asking questions about accidents and sadness. By twelve, she had a drawer full of notebooks and a preference for the quiet corners of the house.

She liked her own company. Always had.

After finishing her tea, she rinsed the mug and left it in the drying rack — one of those small acts that felt more meaningful as time passed. Then she opened the narrow coat closet and stood for a long moment looking at what was left behind.

Tools. Old fishing gear. A coil of rope. A faded green tackle box with a rusted latch. And beneath it all, the metal lip of Granddad's toolbox — the same dented red one he used to haul out whenever the porch door stuck or the motor on the boat wouldn't start.

She tugged it free and carried it to the dining table, which hadn't seen a proper meal in years. A fine coating of dust lifted when she set it down. She wiped the top clean with her sleeve and popped the latches. Inside: pliers, a cracked-handled screwdriver, a stubby pencil sharpened down to the nub. Everything smelled and felt faintly of WD-40.

She ran her fingers across the wrench — the same one she'd held still while Granddad replaced a pipe beneath the kitchen sink. He'd shown her how to brace the pipe with one hand and turn with the other, muttering instructions she only half understood at the time.

The year before he'd taught her how to pull apart an old rotary fan on the porch. They'd spent a whole morning greasing the blades and fitting it back together just like a puzzle. She remembered him handing her a screwdriver and saying, "Nothing's broken on this Earth that can't be fixed with a well-stocked toolbox." She smiled faintly at the memory. Grandad would have hated computers.

Another memory surfaced, uninvited but clear: sitting cross-legged on the floor of the porch while Granddad repaired the screen door. He'd let her hold the jar of screws, telling her each one was a soldier, and she had to make sure none deserted. She remembered how serious she'd taken that job, palms sweaty, until he laughed and ruffled her hair. The sound of that laugh hung in her chest now, just long enough to sting.

Morgan found a loose cabinet hinge in the kitchen and fixed it. Tightened a door pull that had been dangling from one screw. Neither task took more than five minutes, but something in her eased when they were done. It wasn't the result. It was the movement.

She worked without soundtrack. No music. No distractions. Just the sound of the tree branch next to the kitchen window gently brushing against the glass, and the occasional creak in the floorboards.

She returned the tools to the box one by one, wiping each clean with the edge of her shirt. The screwdriver slid into place with a small click. The pencil she kept out, absently running her finger along the bite marks at its base.

She left the box open on the table, lid propped, as though she might need something else from it later.

The house had warmed a little. She could feel it gathering along the floorboards where the sun cut through the east window.

And then it came — not strong, not sudden, but definite. The faintest trace of cigar smoke. Thin and stale, like the echo of a fire long since gone out. Not sharp like a cigarette — heavier, rounder. Rich.

She turned her head slightly toward the living room. Nothing. No movement. No breeze through the cracks. The wind had dropped.

She stood slowly. Walked a quiet loop through the house, into the bedroom, then back toward the fireplace. No ashtray. No smoke. No reason for it.

Still, the scent lingered — not strong, just there.

Morgan paused near the coat closet again and opened it halfway, eyeing the boxes and a few hanging coats inside. Maybe something in there had soaked up the smell. An old jacket. A wool cap tucked away and forgotten. The thought made sense. Almost.

But even as she stood there, the scent was already fading. She didn't chase it. She only breathed it in one last time, an unspoken acknowledgment.

Instead, she walked to the shelf behind the fireplace and scanned the Hemingways — but one of the volumes was slightly out of place. She reached for it — A *Moveable Feast* — and pulled it free. The pages gave off the scent of dry paper and something just slightly bitter.

She flipped through them slowly. No markings. No notes. But a line near the front caught her eye:

"If you are lucky enough to have lived in Paris as a young man, then wherever you go for the rest of your life, it stays with you, for Paris is a moveable feast."

She wondered what her version of Paris might be.

Morgan closed the book and set it gently back on the shelf.

She stood there for a long moment, watching the dust settle where her hand had been.

Then she went back to the kitchen and poured herself a second cup of tea.

By midday, Morgan had opened every cabinet, swept the porch, and cleared the windowsills of a small battalion of dead insects. She worked slowly but steadily, stopping now and then to stretch her back or sip from a glass of water she kept refilling.

She didn't plan her tasks. She just moved from one thing to the next, letting the shape of the house tell her what it needed.

At some point, she set a Hank Williams record on the player and let his voice trail through the cabin like an old friend. The kind of friend who knows which cabinet you keep the good liquor in. The warble in his tone, the crackle of the vinyl — it felt right. Like something the walls remembered.

"I'm So Lonesome I Could Cry."

She didn't tear up, but there was something in the back of her throat that tightened, just for a second.

When the record ended, she didn't change it. Let the quiet come back and settle in.

She passed the bedroom twice during the afternoon. Once to open the shutters. Once just because she was carrying an armful of old blankets she washed to the linen closet.

The bed was still made. Tightly. Like someone had done it years ago and no one had touched it since.

She didn't linger. It still felt like his room. His air. His privacy.

She slept on the couch again that night, without thinking twice about it.

By late the next afternoon, the air had shifted again. The light turned warmer, slanting lower through the porch screens and painting the walls in long, amber stripes.

Morgan sat in the rocker with a cold beer balanced on her knee. Her shirt was damp at the collar from sweat, but she didn't feel the need to change it. She'd worked hard enough to earn it.

The house smelled different now. Less of dust, more of wood and air and whatever had been stirred up during the day. The kitchen window had remained open since morning, and the breeze moved through in slow waves — a steady breath.

She leaned her head back and watched the ceiling for a long moment.

She hadn't thought about her phone all day. She hadn't thought about work, or Atlanta, or whether anyone had noticed she was gone. She was starting to like the feeling.

But with that came a ripple of unease. The Bar was refuge, yes, but it was also witness. These rooms remembered her smaller, her voice higher, her grief newer. She wondered if the house might also remember what she'd tried to forget — the sight of her granddad's empty chair, the way Margaret's eyes had darkened that spring, the stories whispered low so she wouldn't hear. A place can be both comfort and burden.

Records played low in the background — Waylon this time, his voice low and cracked, like a man two drinks deep and just beginning to tell the truth.

Morgan let the albums run their course as the sounds of the marsh turned up their volume. Frogs had started first, one at a time until their calls braided together, followed by the higher trill of crickets in the grass. Farther out, a whip-poor-will cut across the dark with its plaintive rhythm. Once, in the distance, she swore she heard the low thrum of a motorboat shifting gears — but when she stepped onto the porch to listen harder, there was only the vast, layered chorus of the marsh.

She stood, walked the length of the cabin slowly, and paused at the fireplace.

The air in that room felt a little cooler. Not cold — just different than the other rooms.

She glanced toward the rocking chair near the hearth. It hadn't moved. Nothing had changed. But she still looked twice.

Then she lit a candle on the mantle, just because the sun was falling, and returned to the couch as the sky went soft and navy blue.

Somewhere around midnight, Morgan woke without reason.

She wasn't cold. She wasn't thirsty. No noise had startled her. She simply opened her eyes.

The room was very still.

The candle had burned out hours ago, leaving behind a pale wax halo on the mantle. Outside, the marsh had gone dark and deep but not silent — the frogs still murmured, the wind still shifted the trees — but hollowed somehow, like everything had pulled back just slightly to make room for something else.

Morgan stayed on her side, one hand tucked under her cheek, the other resting over her ribs. She didn't reach for her phone. She didn't look at the clock.

She just listened.

A floorboard near the fireplace gave a soft crack. Not loud. Not sharp but enough to make her eyes focus in the dark.

Nothing moved.

Like someone had stood there just moments earlier, watching her sleep.

She sat up slowly, pulling the quilt around her shoulders. The floor felt colder than it had when she lay down, which was natural, though the windows were still shut.

She didn't turn on lamp. The dark felt intact — like a page not to be scribbled on.

She glanced toward the fireplace. The rocking chair was empty, still as the shadows that held it.

She knew that creak hadn't come from her imagination, but old houses make noise. She wasn't about to chase ghosts. Not yet.

"Life in a house after a very long time has to change the space," she thought. "Maybe I'm only hearing the house remembering."

She eased herself back down onto the couch and curled onto her side.

Before her eyes closed again, she whispered one word — not loud, not serious.

"Granddad?" No answer.

Only the marsh. Only the stillness of a house that hadn't forgotten her.

Morning came slowly. Pale light filtered through the porch screens and spilled in long bands across the floor. Once again, the cabin smelled like wood and cotton — something warm, worn, familiar.

Morgan blinked against the soft brightness; arm slung over her eyes. Her pillow had slipped halfway down the couch during the night, but she hadn't stirred much. Her body was still catching up to the rhythm of the place.

She sat up gradually and stretched, the same creak in her spine as yesterday, but it didn't feel like fatigue. It felt like a weight shifting. The kind that might eventually leave.

She stood and moved toward the kitchen; her bare feet quiet against the old floor. The kettle went on without thought. The routine — minimal, domestic — updated muscle memory.

While the water heated, she cracked the screen door open and leaned against the frame. The trees were still damp from the night. A heron moved slow across the far edge of the marsh, half-shadow in the morning fog.

The quiet didn't press this time. It held her gently.

She sipped her tea from the same mug, now rinsed, dried and hers.

There was no schedule. No proof of progress to offer anyone.

But she'd stayed. She'd woken up here again.

And that might be the first true sentence she'd had in a long time.

CHAPTER 4

No one thing alone

Morgan was beginning to find comfort in the sounds and the soft creak of the cabin stretching into morning. It didn't feel foreign anymore—just something she hadn't known she missed. The light in the room was amber and gentle, pooling in the corners like warm honey.

The kettle on the stove began to whistle, but this morning, she reached for coffee instead of tea. She didn't need to calm her nerves. She needed to wake up. She spooned the grounds into the old drip pot, poured the water, and stood still while the dark scent filled the kitchen. For a moment, she listened for something beyond herself—like the house might shift, or the marsh might breathe louder—but all she heard was the faint ticking of the stove and the slow rise of steam.

Mug in hand, she walked over to the record shelf. A worn copy of "The Freewheelin' Bob Dylan" sat near the middle. Morgan tilted her head, wondering who had bought the album or left it behind. Not quite Granddad's style, but she wasn't going to complain.

She placed it on the turntable, set the needle, and let the soft, worn guitar line roll out across the quiet.

"If you're travelin' in the north country fair, where the wind hits heavy on the borderline..."

Morgan smiled faintly, leaning against the kitchen doorway with her mug warm in both hands.

When the second line came—

"Remember me to one who lives there, she once was a true love of mine"

—it caught her just under the ribs.

Ashley.

The name didn't land hard this time. It didn't ache the way it used to. Maybe being here gave her a kind of permission to let herself have that feeling again.

She had worked for years to push it aside, to think of anything else. They'd met in second grade, all awkward elbows and scraped knees, and Morgan had known—even then, before she had words for it—that Ashley was different. She felt different around her.

They'd been close. Always close. Shared sleepovers, notes folded into envelopes, long talks deep into the night.

But the '90s weren't a time for a certain kind of honesty—not in their corner of South Carolina. So the words were never said.

Morgan sipped her coffee, letting the steam cloud her face, and let herself drift back to one of those memories that returned too easily: Ashley leaning against her old Toyota in the high school parking lot, hair pulled back, humming along with the radio. The summer air had smelled of cut grass and gasoline. Morgan remembered the way she'd studied Ashley's profile, sunlight glancing across her cheek, and how badly she'd wanted to hold that moment still. Instead, she had sat behind the wheel, pretending to be distracted by the worn leather of the steering wheel beneath her hands.

The parties were harder. Ashley would always get swept into the center of conversation, laughter circling her like a current. Morgan, by instinct, had drifted to corners, finding empty chairs, nursing warm sodas. Watching but never claiming. Sharing her had been inevitable—Ashley belonged to everyone.

They had kept in touch after high school—late-night texts, letters from college, the occasional phone call when something big happened. But the thread had thinned over the years, until Ashley's name was just part of Margaret's updates. And then, the wedding invitation. Morgan had scheduled herself conveniently out of town on assignment. She hadn't wanted to see the vows. She hadn't wanted to measure herself against them.

Now the song wound on, Dylan's voice soft and stubborn, and she realized her chest wasn't tightening anymore. The ache was present, yes, but dulled—like something worn smooth by years of handling.

It was still early, the kind of time that made the world feel like it belonged only to her.

She stepped onto the porch, letting the screen door clatter behind her, and stood at the railing, coffee in one hand, the day in the other. Outside, the water shimmered silver and gold. An egret stood still as stone at the edge of the grass. Fiddler crabs popped from their burrows, claws raised like tiny flags. The marsh was alive and at ease, and for once, so was she.

That afternoon, Morgan scrubbed the bathroom, cleaned the mirror until it glinted, and opened the closet in the hall just enough to glimpse the clutter waiting inside. The jumble of boxes leaned like a barricade. She shut the door quickly.

Not doing that today.

Instead, she moved back into the kitchen and rummaged through the fridge. The beer she'd picked up from Truluck's was almost gone, tucked behind a jar of pickles and a container of cubed cantaloupe. She opened one, took a sip, and leaned against the counter, letting the cool wash of it settle her.

Then she walked over to the record player again.

"How about a little more Hank?" she murmured with a grin.

She dropped the needle, and the crackle gave way to his familiar drawl.

She didn't mean to dance. But she did. First just a sway, a nod, then a full spin, the bottle still at her lips.

She danced barefoot across the wood floor, hair loose around her shoulders, singing along like the walls were old friends.

She laughed—a real, unguarded laugh that startled her with how it sounded, rusty and light all at once.

And when "Jambalaya" followed, she kept going. She didn't feel like someone avoiding her life anymore.

She just felt like someone alive.

She twirled past the couch, pointed at the broom in the corner like it was a partner, and swung herself into a clumsy two-step that would've made Margaret proud.

The house seemed to echo her laughter back, floorboards humming faintly, windowpanes trembling as though the place itself had been waiting for sound. It didn't feel lonely anymore. It felt... glad.

She ended the dance breathless, leaning against the fricge, the last swallow of beer cool in her hand.

"Okay, Hank," she muttered. "You win."

The floorboards creaked beneath her bare feet, the sound soft and steady, pulling her back to stillness.

Outside, the sun had climbed halfway up the sky. The marsh hummed its steady chorus.

Morgan stepped back onto the porch, holding the empty bottle. She stood on the top step and pressed her bare heel gently into the third board. It bowed just enough to remind her.

Tomorrow, she thought. She'd go into town. Check the hardware store, maybe see Ashley's dad. That place had been in their family for generations. She'd need supplies anyway—if she meant to stay, the porch would have to be sound.

She could stretch it out, turn it into an errand. Stop for gas and groceries. Maybe.

She didn't feel like she was hiding anymore.

She twisted the cap from another beer just as the sun began to lean westward.

By the time the fireflies appeared, blinking along the edge of the porch, the house had fallen still again. But the stillness felt different now. Not like waiting.

Like belonging.

She left the porch light off and let the darkness settle. And when she lay down on the couch later, quilt pulled up to her chin, she whispered something to the room without thinking.

"Thanks for the dance."

No one answered. Of course no one answered. But the silence felt steady, almost attentive.

And she smiled anyway.

CHAPTER 5

The world breaks everyone

Morgan was halfway through her second cup of coffee when the delivery truck came rattling up the drive. She heard it before she saw it—the deep, unfamiliar hum that didn't belong in the usual chorus of frogs, wind, and far-off gulls. She set her mug down, brushed her hands against her jeans, and stepped to the porch.

"Morning," the driver called, setting down two large cardboard boxes with a polite nod.

She raised her mug in a little toast. "Thank you, sir."

The boxes weren't heavy. One was marked with fresh UPS tape, the other with her own faded handwriting from a move years ago: WINTER STUFF / MISC. She recognized it immediately. Claire's handiwork.

Morgan crouched and traced her finger along the seam of the first box before carrying it inside. Claire had promised she'd handle it—send what Morgan asked for. Mostly clothes, a few comforts. And, true to form, she had volunteered to stay in Morgan's Atlanta apartment while she was gone. Said it saved her from subletting something during the fumigation drama in her building—"fumigated or fumigated-adjacent," Claire had joked, depending on which day the landlord decided to answer emails.

Inside the first box were carefully rolled T-shirts, jeans, socks matched in neat pairs, and a zip-up hoodie Morgan thought she'd lost years ago. She suspected Claire had it the whole time. Tucked beneath the clothes was a smaller carton holding the portable satellite WiFi system Morgan used for work travel. She turned it over in her hands, considering. At some point, she might decide to set it up, check in, and make sure the rest of the world was still out there.

At the very bottom, wrapped in a striped kitchen towel, was the little ceramic dish she used for sea salt. Chipped on one edge, clumsy with glaze, the uneven blue paint showing the thumbprint of an 8-year-old. She had made it in third grade for Granddad. He'd set it on his kitchen counter and used it daily, declaring it "finer than the Waterford crystal." Morgan held it for a long moment, thumb tracing the flaw, before placing it gently on the stove.

The second box was more of the same—flannel pajamas, worn sweaters, a pair of slippers she hadn't worn in years. At the bottom were books she hadn't asked for but was glad to see: a battered copy of *The Sun Also Rises*, a thick volume of short stories, and a paperback mystery Claire must have thrown in just for fun. Wrapped in bubble wrap was a framed photo from their office Christmas party two years ago: she and Claire, both wearing cheap reindeer antlers and holding mugs of mulled wine, caught between sarcasm and surrender. A sticky note was taped to the glass:

Be good to yourself, even if you don't deserve it. —C.

Morgan smiled faintly. She didn't always love Claire's timing, but she appreciated her aim.

She broke down the boxes and leaned them against the hall closet, which, as usual, refused to close all the way. The door bounced back like it objected having the boxes lean against it. She pressed it shut and left it.

It felt good to have pieces of her other life here—threadbare comforts, the clutter of the familiar. Still, she needed fresh things. A shower washed the morning from her skin. She tugged on one of the T-shirts Claire had sent, brushed a hand through her damp hair until it looked halfway presentable, and pulled on her jacket.

Good enough.

Her appetite was climbing with the sun. She decided to drive back to Truluck's for groceries, detergent, beer, and—most importantly—one of the breakfast sandwiches that had become their quiet local culinary masterpiece.

The drive into town was short, marsh grasses sweeping along the two-lane road, the smell of brine and pine mingling in the cool air. Truluck's sat squat and unassuming at the bend, the same chipped Coca-Cola sign leaning out front, the parking lot gravel worn into ruts. She pushed the door open and stepped into a place that smelled like coffee, cured meat, and the faint tang of bleach.

The cooler against the back wall was new—taller, humming steady, packed with white-paper parcels of local bacon and thick-cut ribeyes. She took both. Tonight the dining room table would hold a proper dinner, probably the first in years.

At the counter she ordered the breakfast sandwich, watching as Mr. Truluck's daughter built it with a kind of craftsman's pride: bread toasted just enough to offer perfect support, bacon chewy but lean, a fried egg with edges crisped in butter, and a single slice of melting American cheese that glued the whole thing together. The first bite was heavenly.

She gathered a basket with detergent, vegetables, a bag of yellow onions, and a carton of fresh tomatoes. She lingered over the jarred goods, finally adding a jar of pickled carrots just because. The clink of glass settled into her bag, a counterpoint to the muffled thud of beer bottles.

When she stepped outside, the sun was climbing past the tree line. She turned toward the car—and stopped.

There, in an old rocking chair on the porch, sat Mr. Truluck himself. His cane leaned against the armrest, and his eyes, clouded with age, blinked behind lenses thick as old jars.

"Mr. Truluck?" Morgan said softly.

He turned his head, slow as a tide. "Well now," he rasped. "Who's voice is that?"

"It's Morgan," she said, moving closer. "Langford."

A smile cracked his face, thin but certain. "Bill's grandchild."

"That's right."

"Oh my goodness. When did you get home? You stayin' awhile?"

"Visiting. Taking care of some things around the cabin."

He chuckled, a sound like gravel shifting. "The old Bar. Lord, the times we had there. Oyster roasts, pig pickins, card games ran so long we had to bring out lanterns. Your granddaddy was the best of company.

Loud, funny, always with a story. He once showed me how to fix a spark plug—or maybe I showed him. His chair creaked once, twice. "We sat out there just a few days before... well. He was talking about you. Said he couldn't believe how grown you were. Said he was lookin' forward to your birthday, wanted to see your smile that day."

Morgan tilted her head. Granddad had died on February 20th. Her birthday wasn't until May. Maybe the old man was mistaken. Time got loose when you were near ninety.

He scratched his cheek. "Well, maybe I got that wrong. Could've been another plan he was making."

She gave a faint smile, though something in her chest flickered.

The old man's eyes softened. "He was proud of you, Morgan. Told me more than once. Said you were sharp. Said you'd do somethin' good in the world."

Her hand rested lightly on the porch rail. "Thank you, Mr. Truluck. That means a lot to me."

"You come by anytime you like. Tell Margaret I said hey."

"I will."

She walked back to her car, the glass clink of carrots and beer echoing in the quiet. That evening she cooked the ribeye with butter and garlic, the smell filling the cabin until it felt like a new kind of homecoming. She sat at the dining table, a glass of beer beside her, savoring each bite. She hadn't made herself a dinner like that in months—maybe years.

Afterwards she rinsed the plate, wiped the counter, and finally gave in to setting up the WiFi. The small modem blinked to life, filling the air with an invisible tether to the world. She checked her phone—emails, news headlines, a message from Claire reminding her to eat something green. Morgan laughed, sent back a thumbs-up emoji, and closed it.

Wrapped in the old blanket she'd washed earlier in the week, she stretched on the couch. The rocking chair sat still in its corner. She let her eyes close.

She woke just past midnight. The room was dim and hushed, She lay still until she realized what she was hearing—the slow, steady creak of wood.

The rocking chair was moving.

Back and forth.

Back and forth.

Morgan blinked hard, tried to clear her vision, but the chair kept on. In her drowsy haze, she thought she could see a figure there—not solid, not lit, but a suggestion of shoulders, the bent line of someone seated. A silhouette that shifted when she tried to focus.

She didn't sit up. Didn't even breathe deeply. She whispered, soft as a thought:

"Granddad? Are you with me?" The chair stopped.

The hush of the house pressed in, steady and immense. Morgan stayed still a long time, her pulse a heavy drum. Every part of her told her she hadn't been dreaming, but what else could it have been?

At last she rolled to her side, pulling the blanket to her chin. Her heartbeat slowed. Sleep returned, though thin and uneasy.

By morning, the cabin was itself again, golden light spreading through the kitchen, shadows stretching long. She brewed coffee, rinsed the pan from the steak, and on a scrap of paper started a list:

Stuff for porch step.

She tucked it under a magnet on the fridge.

Then she stacked records on the changer and pushed play. The Tams crackled to life, "Be Young, Be Foolish, Be Happy" carrying through the rooms. The sound tugged her backward—sunburnt spring breaks, cheap tanning lotion, Garden City arcade. She hummed along while folding towels, wiping down the fridge, letting the music fill spaces she hadn't realized were hollow.

The Bar wasn't just holding her now. It was being filled by her—one song, one list, one breath at a time.

CHAPTER 6

We are all apprentices

Morgan felt the third step give just a little too much beneath her heel.

She paused mid-step, coffee in hand, and rocked back slightly. The board bowed in the center, just enough to be a problem. A fine crack had begun to spider outward, almost invisible unless you were looking for it.

She crouched, set her mug on the porch rail, and pressed her thumb into the wood. It gave — soft, compliant.

She tested the others.

Gonna do one. Might as well do all three.

She sighed and stood, taking a sip from her mug. The porch was sound, but the steps had done their job for one too many rainy seasons.

Inside, she rinsed the mug and tied her hair back. Her boots were still by the door, dusty from yesterday's wandering. She pulled them on, grabbed the ring of shed keys from the bowl, and made her way around the side of the house.

The shed door stuck a little, but gave with a shove. Inside, the air was thick with the smell of motor oil, mildew, and many slow seasons. Granddad's larger toolbox was still where it had always been, right beneath the low shelf where old paint cans gathered dust. She opened it, checked the hammer, the nails, the brackets.

She had the hardware.

What she didn't have was the lumber.

She looked once more around the shed, hoping for spare boards tucked behind something — but no luck. Everything was either warped, broken, or too short.

That settled it.

She stepped out into the sunlight and brushed her hands clean on the thighs of her jeans. It was time to go a bit farther into town.

The marsh flanked the road in long, open breaths. Trees thinned, signs sharpened. Civilization gathered slowly — mailboxes, clapboard churches, the soft pulse of a working day already in motion.

Harbor Iron & Tool sat at the end of Main — small, square, and dependable. The old sign had been freshly hand-painted, the screen door no longer sun-warped and stubborn. Morgan hadn't stepped foot inside in years, but nothing about it looked particularly unfamiliar.

She parked under the shade of a leaning pecan tree and walked toward the entrance, her boots catching grit on the pavement.

The scent met her in an instant — wood shavings, iron filings, the mineral tang of fertilizer. She stopped for a second and let it settle. For a moment she could have been an eight-year-old girl again. Fetching sandpaper for Granddad. Slipping dimes he gave her into the large, round bubblegum machine beside the front door.

Morgan made her way toward the back, past pegboard hooks lined with screwdrivers, gloves, and saw blades. She found the lumber rack near the rear wall and ran a hand along a stack of pressure-treated planks, checking for bowing and knots. They weren't cheap, but they were straight and clean.

She picked out four 2x6 boards and turned to walk toward the counter.

And all of a sudden there she was.

Ashley.

Behind the register. Hair a little longer. Rolled sleeves. A pencil tucked behind one ear.

She was laughing at something the older man across from her said — a customer, probably a regular — and then she looked up.

Their eyes met.

Ashley's face stilled for a beat. Then softened.

"Morgan," she said, smiling.

Morgan blinked, caught between surprise and something older — a feeling she hadn't expected to feel so quickly. Especially today.

"Ashley," she said, adjusting the boards in her arms. "Hey."

Ashley stepped out from behind the counter, wiping her hands on a shop rag.

"Replacing the porch steps out at The Bar," Morgan said.

There was a brief pause — warm, but uncertain. Ashley shifted her weight slightly, then asked,

"So... are you back-back?"

Morgan shook her head. "For now. Just trying to help out for a while. When did you come back?"

Ashley smiled and nodded. "Well, that's a story for another time."

She stepped forward and gave Morgan a hug.

There were hugs — and then there were Ashley hugs. She had always hugged Morgan like she hadn't seen her in years. She never let go first.

Morgan breathed her in before she could stop herself — detergent, sawdust, something floral that had to be shampoo. Her arms ached to hold on, but she forced herself to ease back when Ashley finally did.

"It's so good to see you," Ashley said, slipping behind the counter again. "You still have the same number?"

"I do."

"Good. I'll text you."

"Please... stop by any time you're out that way."

Morgan paid, shouldered her boards and gave a small wave as she headed for the door.

The bell above the frame jingled a happy goodbye.

Outside, the air held a chill that worked its way under her jacket and down her sleeves. The sun was up, but it didn't warm much yet — just lit the tops of the trees and made the dew on her windshield glitter like frost.

Morgan loaded the boards into the back of the truck, careful not to scuff the edges, and closed the tailgate with a soft thud. Her breath fogged in the cold, briefly hanging between her and the quiet street.

The town looked the same — sleepy, sunlit, still tucked into the edges of winter. Nothing loud about it. Just porches and pickup trucks and the kind of silence that came from people knowing where everyone else lived. Hell, where everyone's great-grandparents had lived for that matter.

She climbed in and turned the key. The engine coughed once, then settled into a steady hum. As she pulled away from the curb, her fingers tapped lightly on the steering wheel.

Ashley.

She had not seen that coming. The way her voice had landed, just the same. The way she hadn't changed. And had.

Morgan kept her eyes on the road, but her mind looped the moment — the way Ashley had hugged her. Like it wasn't for show. Like it was just what you do when someone who matters walks back into the room.

The heater finally softened the air inside the cabin.

She drove slowly.

Not out of hesitation.

But because, for the first time in a long time, she didn't feel the need to rush.

Back at The Bar, the afternoon had turned sharp with wind. Morgan opened the passenger door and stood for a minute, letting the cold nudge against her collarbones. The sky had that brittle look it got sometimes in March — pale blue and thin, like a robin's eggshell.

She unloaded the boards one at a time and leaned them against the inside porch wall. Each one thudded softly as it met the wood, the sound clean and certain. It felt good to carry something solid. Tomorrow, she would finish the steps.

Morgan didn't eat dinner right away. She pulled some of the firewood and decided to let the electric heat take a break tonight. She lit her first fire in the old stone fireplace, letting the warmth stretch into the corners of the room.

The light outside had gone dim, that last soft dip before full dark. She flipped on the lamp near the window and let it cast its amber glow across the floorboards.

For a moment, she stood in the middle of the room, listening.

Not for anything in particular.

Just listening.

The house made its usual sounds — a pop in the wall paneling, a soft creak above the hallway.

She cued up some records — something she hadn't heard before — and let the old console run. The needle dropped with a crackle, and then came Chet Baker, soft and smooth. A slow trumpet line, easy and clean, like it had taken its time getting here.

While the music played, she made something quick. Leftover steak and a baked potato. A splash of red wine from the bottle Claire had packed in her box, though Morgan hadn't noticed it until today. She almost texted to say thanks. Almost.

Later, wrapped in her blanket with her plate cleared and the record player hissing toward silence, she leaned back into the corner of the couch and stared into the fire.

No words. No effort to conjure anything.

Just warmth and wood. The steady sound of the ending day.

Morgan didn't remember drifting off.

One minute she was watching the fire. The next, her eyes were open again and the room had changed. Not dramatically. Just enough to notice.

The fire had burned low — no flames, only a slow orange pulse beneath the logs. The air had cooled. And the cabin felt... different.

She didn't move right away. Stayed under the quilt, still and quiet, eyes adjusting to the dark.

That's when she noticed the chair.

It wasn't rocking.

But it looked off. Shifted slightly — like it had been moved, just a little. The kind of shift that doesn't happen accidentally.

And then came the sound.

A soft creak. Just one. Then another.

Back and forth.

She didn't speak. Didn't sit up.

She only stared.

The chair moved slowly. Gently. As if to not wake her fully.

Morgan's hand twitched under the quilt, halfway to pushing herself upright, halfway to pulling the blanket higher. She hesitated. If she stood, she'd have to face it. If she stayed down, maybe it would pass.

And from the far side near the window she heard music.

It was low and a bit muffled, like hearing music from another room. A single, brushed guitar chord. And then, Willie Nelson's voice — soft and clean, full of air and ache.

"Sometimes I wonder why I spend the lonely nights..."

She didn't sit up. Didn't stop it. Just listened. Maybe she'd grabbed it by mistake.

Morgan didn't remember pulling that one. She didn't even remember seeing it.

But "Stardust" played anyway.

By morning, the fire had gone out completely. Only a faint curl of ash sat in the belly of the hearth. Morgan stirred beneath the quilt, blinked once into the light, and let herself wake slowly.

The chair was still again. The cabin silent.

She rose quietly, feet bare against the cold floor, and crossed slowly to the HiFi. Morgan raised the wooden lid of the console but there was no record on the platter. None loaded onto the changing arm. No record un-sleeved.

She lowered the lid and stood still for a moment, her hand resting on the wood. If she hadn't been so tired, she might have sworn it was real. And stranger still, after checking the sleeves twice, she realized something else: "Stardust" wasn't in Granddad's collection.

The thought landed heavy. Comfort and unease in equal measure.

While the water heated, she tidied what little remained from the night before. Folded the blanket. Stacked the plate and wine glass near the sink.

She didn't try to make sense of it. She had been tired and half asleep. That was explanation enough.

When the kettle hissed, Morgan made her tea and carried it to the porch. She sat in the rocker and pulled the blanket around her shoulders.

A thin layer of mist hovered just above the grass. The marsh was slow to wake.

She sipped once. Breathed in the cool.

She sipped again. Let the quiet settle.

The neighbor must have been playing music on his porch. It was colder last night. Sound travels farther in the cold.

CHAPTER 7

A Kiss To Build A Dream On

Granddad had provided zero frills with these porch stairs. Morgan shook her head and smiled.

Just rough planks and nails, wood meant to hold up under work boots and muddy soles. The boards didn't look worse than yesterday. But Morgan could see it clearly — the sag where the middle dipped with weight, the faint split just starting to travel along the grain.

She pressed her boot to the edge of the step and shifted her weight forward. It held, but only just.

She stepped back.

The sun hadn't fully cleared the trees yet, and the marsh was still wearing its morning silver. Morgan sipped her coffee and considered her next move. She had the tools — she'd left the hammer and pry bar on the kitchen counter. The new boards leaned against the porch wall, exactly where she'd dropped them the day before. Dry enough not to warp, strong enough not to go through this ritual again anytime soon.

She set her mug on the windowsill and crouched to start pulling the nails.

They each came loose with a groan that made her think of bones realigning. The old wood resisted in places, like it had grown used to being part of the house and didn't want to leave.

She understood that feeling.

By the time she'd removed the damaged boards, smoothed away the splinters, and pulled the dead grass underneath, the sun had climbed high enough to reach the top of her shoulders. She stood and stretched, back popping once, then twice. A smear of dirt ran across her forearm where she'd brushed her hand absentmindedly.

Morgan liked small work — a task with a beginning, a middle, and an end.

She was halfway through measuring the fit on the next step when she heard the crunch of tires on sandy dirt.

Morgan looked up.

A small silver SUV had turned into the drive — not fast, but certain, like it had done so a hundred times. Her stomach did a slow turn, not unpleasant.

The car stopped. The door opened.

Ashley stepped out.

She shaded her eyes with one hand and smiled, easy and familiar.

"I figured you might be out here."

Morgan stood and dusted her palms on the back of her jeans. "Well, I'm trying to keep Margaret from falling through the stairs here. Can you imagine?"

Ashley walked slowly toward the porch, gaze flicking to the tools, the scattered nails, the new boards resting at a slight angle.

"It's looking good," she said. "Better than I remember it, honestly."

"Yeah, that's all me."

Ashley laughed — low and genuine. "I'm sure."

Morgan stepped down from the porch. She gestured toward the rocker nearest the railing. "You want to sit for a bit? Cup of coffee?"

Ashley nodded and settled in with that same quiet confidence she'd always had.

"I hope I'm not interrupting," she said.

"Not at all," Morgan replied as she stepped inside to reach for another mug.

Ashley leaned back slightly in the chair. "Well, I'm glad I caught you. I was coming out to see if you were up for a mildly dull but definitely delicious evening at my parents' house."

Morgan raised an eyebrow. "What's going on?"

"Daddy's doing a Low Country Boil next month. My folks would love to see you. And I thought maybe… if you were up for it… might want to come."

The wind shifted slightly, carrying in the briny scent of the marsh. Morgan stood still for a beat too long.

"Wow… Low Country Boil, huh?" she said. "Haven't done that in years."

"Well," Ashley said, voice softening, "then it might be time."

Morgan nodded slowly. "That sounds… good. Yeah. I'd like that."

Ashley smiled, and for a moment, it was the same as when they were fifteen — sunshine and heat and so many things left unsaid. Ashley's name still tasted like summer — and heartache.

They sat in the kind of silence that came easy between people who knew what not to say. Then, slowly, they started to talk about family.

"So, tell me... how did you end up back home?"

Ashley exhaled, eyes going out toward the marsh trying to find the right way to begin the conversation. "Well... that was one of those long, hard decisions that had to be made overnight."

She gave a short laugh. "My dad needed to retire, and after that heart procedure last year, it was clear he couldn't run the day-to-day anymore. You probably heard that part."

"I did," Morgan said. "Margaret told me."

"Yeah, well... that was half of it."

Ashley tucked a strand of hair behind her ear, her smile wry now. "The other half was realizing my marriage was done, and I was tired of pretending otherwise."

Morgan kept her face still, listening.

"We'd been drifting for years," Ashley went on. "It wasn't anything dramatic at first — no big fights, no scandal. Just two people moving in very different directions. But then there was the booze."

Her voice lowered, steady but sharp at the edges. "He liked it too much. It began every night, just before supper, and over the years it became a constant in his hand. I couldn't stand it — the smell of it, the way it turned him mean or blank depending on the day."

"I mean, we always drank beer. At the beach, out with friends — that felt easy. Normal. But this was different. This was a whole other world, and I didn't want to live in it."

A thought moved quick and quiet through Morgan's mind — Ashley never seeing a bourbon bottle tucked away in the kitchen. It was more of an instinct than a thought.

Ashley's gaze stayed out toward the water. "When he took a position in Charlotte, I thought maybe the distance would fix us or he would begin to miss me, at least, give us a break. Instead, it just gave him a new city to drink in."

"And so you came home," Morgan said softly.

"I came home," Ashley nodded. "At first it felt like failure. You know how people around here can be. Divorce is still a word whispered over coffee or gossiped on at Bridge club."

A small shrug. "But the more I stood behind that counter at the store, the more it felt like mine. Daddy had built something steady. Familiar. And for once, I didn't feel like I was trying to fit myself into somebody else's story. I could write my own, right there in a place that was familiar but needed some TLC."

Morgan let the words settle. "Are you happy there?"

"I am," Ashley said. "I've made some changes — swapped out that old wooden cash register for something with a screen, added a few things online. But I still know every customer by name, still smell like sawdust most days. It feels... happy. And that's worth a lot."

"I'm really glad you stayed and it's yours. Selfishly it's comforting for me to know it's still in the family and you're doing something you love."

"Thanks, Morgan." Ashley gave the smile she reserved for the happiest of moments.

"I need to get going. I'll text you the details about the boil," Ashley said, standing and handing Morgan her mug.

They stood facing each other for a moment, the space between them filled with their own shared memories. Ashley's smile softened, and she stepped forward.

"I'm so glad you're back," she said. Then, without hesitation, she leaned in with a big hug and kissed Morgan gently on the cheek — not quick, not lingering, just certain.

Morgan didn't move. Didn't pull away. She let the warmth of it land.

Ashley stepped back. "See you soon? Maybe you can tell me a little more about why you're back too."

"Yeah," Morgan said, voice quiet. "Definitely. I'll see you "

Ashley turned and walked to her car. The tires crunched slowly down the drive until the sound faded into wind and birdsong.

Morgan stayed standing at the edge of the porch. She reached up and touched her cheek, as if the imprint might still be there.

Then, from inside the house, a sound.

She turned, slowly.

From the far corner, Louis Armstrong's voice filled the room, warm and golden.

"Give me a kiss to build a dream on..."

Morgan stepped into the doorway. She hadn't touched the turntable that morning. Hadn't even looked at it.

"And my imagination will thrive upon that kiss."

The song swelled, but it was the same muted sound that Stardust had. Almost like the speakers were out of phase... or it was coming through the wall.

She didn't move. This song was playing itself.

Morgan stood there, the song curling softly through the room like smoke. The voice was gravel and gold, the kind that could stitch together a morning with a memory.

She walked over slowly, knelt by the player, and just listened.

Her hand went to her phone. Jimmy was Morgan's favorite cousin and the one closest to her in age. She hadn't seen him since she got back into town and he just happened to be a contractor, so this would be one of those convenient situations that come along on rare occasions.

Jimmy picked up on the third ring. "Hey cousin, you good? I was wondering when I'd hear from you! You know Aunt Margaret can't keep a secret for more than a week but she threatened me with death if I called you first."

Morgan smiled. "It's good to hear your voice and you are welcome to stop by any time. I was actually going to ask if you minded swinging by when you get a chance? I need help figuring something out with this old HiFi. It's doing weird stuff and I think it may be a short."

"Sure," he said. "Be there in a bit."

By the time he knocked and stepped inside, the music had long quieted. The stereo sat silent. Nothing on, nothing humming. He gave Morgan the big bear hug she always looked forward to and then walked over to the console and crouched beside it. In one hand six brown bottles in a cardboard holder. The clink of glass followed him in like punctuation.

"This old thing still got the radio wired in?"

"I think so," she said. "I just wanted to make sure the place didn't burn down."

He tapped the side gently. "Could be a short. Sometimes old radios pick up bleed from other signals. Weather bands, even truckers if the antenna's still wired to the chimney."

"You think truckers are broadcasting Louis Armstrong?"

Jimmy shrugged. "Stranger things have happened. Static gets weird out here. Especially with these old wires."

He opened the receiver cabinet, jiggled a couple of knobs, sniffed the air.

"No heat. No signal. Nothing playing now."

Morgan stood behind him, arms crossed, watching the room like it might give a clue.

Jimmy closed the cabinet and straightened up. "It was more than likely just a fluke," he said.

Morgan nodded slowly, though her eyes didn't move from the stereo. "Yeah. You're probably right."

Jimmy stayed for about an hour. Just long enough to make sure Morgan was settled and the beer he had brought with him was cold enough. It was.

Once she was alone Morgan did the only thing she knew to do. She got back to work.

The boards fit snug, almost like the porch had been waiting to accept them. She double-checked the alignment, braced the edges, and began driving in the nails — slow, steady, measured.

Each strike echoed faintly through the quiet.

She liked the rhythm of it.

By the time the last one sank flush into the grain, her hands were sore and her shoulders ached in that good, earned kind of way. She sat back on her heels and looked at the steps. They weren't perfect, but they were solid.

That was enough.

She stood, stretched, and walked back inside, wiping sweat from her brow with the sleeve of her shirt.

Morgan washed her hands in the kitchen sink and opened the window above it, letting the midday breeze move through. Somewhere out in the marsh, a bird called once, then again — sharp and lonely.

She dried her hands, poured a glass of water, and walked it to the porch. She sat in the rocker letting her bare feet settle onto the newly repaired step.

She took a long sip and let the glass rest against her chest.

Ashley's voice echoed softly in her memory. *I'm glad you're back.*

Morgan couldn't remember the last time she didn't flinch at the thought of being seen.

She leaned her head against the back of the chair. The wood felt warm from the sun.

Inside, the silence remained.

But it didn't feel empty.

It felt like The Bar was waiting to see what she'd do next.

She stayed in the rocker until the glass went warm in her hand and the light on the marsh began to tilt westward. The wind picked up slightly, just enough to move the Spanish moss along the branches like exhaling.

When she finally stood, her legs had stiffened, but it felt good to stretch. She stepped back into the house and paused in the doorway, listening.

Still no sound. No movement.

Morgan walked back to the kitchen and set the glass in the sink. Then she turned, eyes drawn to the fireplace.

The rocking chair by the hearth was still again, the space around it unchanged.

She walked over slowly, half-expecting to feel something — a shift in the air, a trace of warmth. But there was nothing. Just the chair, still as it had always been.

She reached down and gently rocked it once, watching it move back, then forward, then settle.

"Alright, now," she said softly, almost like she was speaking to the chair itself. Or to something just past it.

Then she turned away and opened the back door, letting the air pass through the house from front to back in a clean, straight line.

She swept the floors, humming a little as she went — not a song she knew, just something that matched the rhythm of her steps. The day had taken shape in ways she hadn't expected. She hadn't planned for Ashley. Certainly hadn't planned for a house DJ.

But here she was.

By the time the sun slipped behind the trees, she'd made a sandwich and poured a beer to go with it.

After dinner, she left the dishes in the sink and stepped back onto the porch. The sky was lavender now, shading slowly into blue. A few stars had started to blink awake overhead.

She sat on the top step and leaned her arms on her knees.

She traced the smooth edge with one finger, still warm from the sun.

The night settled in layers — the first few frogs, then the soft whine of insects, then the occasional splash out in the reeds. All of it rising and falling like breath.

Morgan closed her eyes for a moment.

She could still feel the shape of Ashley's presence. That quiet, grounded way she had of showing up — like she was never in a rush to be anywhere else.

It didn't feel unfinished, the way things had between them years ago.

It felt buried but not broken.

The marsh wind shifted again, and she caught it — faint, familiar — the smell of cigar smoke.

Her eyes opened.

It wasn't strong. Just enough to notice. Enough to know it didn't come from outside.

She stood slowly, scanning the yard, the trees, the empty road.

Nothing.

She stepped back inside. The scent was gone. The chair was still.

But she didn't doubt what she'd smelled.

She just said quietly to the room, "Okay," then sighed.

She turned off the lights and settled onto the couch beneath her quilt.

Sleep didn't come quickly, but it wasn't restless either. Morgan lay on her side beneath the quilt, watching the flicker of porch light shadows dance faintly across the ceiling. The night was soft.

The chair hadn't moved. The music hadn't played again.

But the message had landed.

She wasn't alone here but she wasn't afraid of that anymore. Not in the way she thought.

Morgan slept deeply that night and woke before sunrise. A steady, even quiet held the house like the moment before a bell rings.

Morgan slipped out from under the quilt and walked barefoot into the kitchen. She moved without turning on any lights. Lit the stove. Filled the kettle. The routine settled in her hands like it had always been there.

As the water warmed, she opened the back door and stepped outside.

The marsh was wrapped in fog, the kind that softened everything — trees, sky, horizon — into one shared breath. Even the air felt suspended.

She sat on the step and held her coffee in both hands, watching the white lift in slow, invisible threads.

She didn't speak. Didn't move more than she had to. Just breathed and listened.

The porch creaked once behind her.

But she didn't turn around.

When the fog finally began to pull back from the marsh, it did so in slow ribbons, revealing water and reeds and the faintest blush of dawn behind the trees. Morgan stood and stretched, her spine giving a soft crack.

She went back inside and set the mug in the sink.

Today would be quiet. Maybe she'd clean the closet. Maybe not. She'd see how the hours moved.

Before getting dressed, she walked over to the bookcase and ran her fingers along the line of Hemingway spines. Her hand stopped at *A Moveable Feast*, but she didn't pull it down this time. She just touched it, steady, like she was letting someone know she saw it.

Then she turned and reached for her notebook — one of the older ones Claire had sent, the kind with soft, weathered pages and a little ink smudge on the corner.

She sat at the table.

Opened it.

And started to write.

CHAPTER 8

A clean, well lighted place

The fire had gone out overnight, leaving only a soft layer of ash in the hearth and the faint scent of woodsmoke still clinging to the room. Morgan woke early, not startled—gently released from sleep.

She lay still for a while, just watching the light make its slow climb across the wall. A calm light. Pale, but every day showing clearer signs that warm spring was coming.

When she finally stood, the floor was still cool under her feet. She moved through the house without turning on a single lamp. No need.

Her notebook was still on the table.

She ran her palm   the cover, then opened it again. The lines she'd written the night before looked steadier than she remembered. Not brilliant, but not bad.

She smiled faintly. Closed it. Let it sit.

The air was crisper—clear and sharp. Out over the marsh, a single heron drifted above the fog, its wings cutting a slow, perfect path.

Morgan watched it go, barefoot on the wooden threshold.

She didn't speak. She didn't need to.

She started a load of laundry—mostly flannels and jeans—and opened a few windows to let the air cycle through. The house smelled like sleep and ash and salt.

She didn't mind it. She left the door cracked just enough to hear the wind move through the trees.

After breakfast, she wiped down the counters and swept the kitchen floor. The light outside had that strange, silvery brightness March sometimes brought—just one of those days between cold and bloom.

She made a short list of groceries she might pick up later—coffee, bread, maybe eggs if Truluck's had received a delivery.

She stood for a while by the kitchen window, watching two squirrels chase each other across the yard. The marsh was louder today—more frogs, more birdsong, more presence. Like it had decided, too, that maybe it was time to wake up.

Back at the table, Morgan opened the notebook once more. This time she jotted a few uneven lines. Not a story. Not even sentences. More like fragments. Words that came without pressure: salt, porch light, Ashley's smile, the smell of rain. She let them sit there, shapeless but alive, and closed the book again before the urge to judge them could take hold.

She flipped back a few pages and tried again. This time the fragments leaned longer.

"Porch light still burning. Boots lined by the door. Her voice low when she said my name." She stared at the words. They weren't much, but they tugged at memory — nights with Granddad sitting on the porch in near-dark, or Ashley leaning in on the couch when they were teenagers, whispering a joke no one else would understand. She tapped her pen once against the margin, then set it down before the pressure of turning fragments into full sentences made her feel anxious.

By early afternoon, Morgan was out on the porch again, sanding the edges of the steps she'd replaced. Enough to smooth the corners and take the bite off the grain. She worked slowly, rhythmically, the block of sandpaper hissing across the wood with each pass.

There was something deeply satisfying about it— the transformation of something rough into something useful. No need for inspiration, no pressure to get it perfect. Just a little time and attention.

When she stopped to stretch, she noticed the clouds beginning to drift in from the east, soft-edged and high. A colder wind pressed in behind them. She stepped back inside, peeled off her hoodie, and poured a glass of water.

As she sipped, she looked at the chair by the hearth.

It was behaving.

But something about its stillness made her feel watched in a way that wasn't threatening.

She didn't say anything. Just nodded at it like she might acknowledge an old dog too tired to get up from the rug.

Back at the table, she scribbled in the margin of her notebook. Shapes of ideas. A scrap of dialogue. A memory of Granddad. She didn't pressure herself to make them into more. Not yet.

She caught herself writing Ashley's name again, almost without thinking. The letters looped across the page, a little unsteady, as if her hand remembered something her mind was trying not to. Morgan pressed her palm flat across the word until the ink smudged, then turned the page. She thought: Ashley doesn't need to know about the bourbon. That part of her life was her own. But the thought carried weight, more than she wanted to admit.

By late afternoon, the sky had thickened into a low sheet of gray. Morgan pulled the last of the warm laundry from the dryer—flannels, socks, a couple of T-shirts—and folded them on the back of the couch.

The washer and dryer, a pair of old Kenmore machines in the golden harvest hue from the mid-'70s, still rumbled along like champions. Granddad used to say they'd "outlive the house and most the family." So far, he hadn't been wrong. No high-efficiency digital screen could match the way those machines got dirt out of clothes or dried them so thoroughly they burned your hands a little when you removed them from the dryer.

She turned on the lamp by the window. The light fell soft against the floorboards, stretching shadows in all directions. She didn't mind the gray outside. It made the house feel closer somehow—more of a world in itself.

Ashley's visit was still with her. She didn't try to name what she felt. Just let it settle the way the day had, without needing to be anything more than it was.

She thought of the cheek kiss, the way Ashley's voice had softened on the porch. The words replayed in her head — "I'm glad you're back." A simple phrase, but Morgan kept circling it, wondering if Ashley had meant more. Wondering if Ashley still thought of them as the girls who used to fall asleep mid-conversation, a whole night gone in whispers. The thought stirred something tender and sharp at the same time. She pushed it down with the neat folding of an old flannel shirt.

The clouds finally opened up just after dusk.

Not hard. Not in sheets. Just a steady tapping against the tin porch roof and a fine mist that turned the screens silver. Morgan stood just inside the doorway, watching the drops hit the edge of the steps. They darkened with the wet but held their shape, firm and level, no pooling at the seams.

Inside, she lit the fire, more for comfort than warmth. The temperature had dipped, but not dramatically. Just enough that the flicker of flame gave the room a warm heartbeat.

She curled up on the couch with a book she'd picked out earlier—the short stories again. Not from the beginning. Just wherever the book wanted to open.

She didn't read long. The words blurred after a few pages, her mind drifting to Ashley's voice, the way she'd looked on the porch. It was a very intimate feeling to share a long history and memory with someone like that.

Morgan set the book down on her chest and closed her eyes.

The rain softened against the roof. A pop from the fire cracked the quiet.

Then a floorboard creaked—faint, familiar.

She didn't open her eyes. She let the moment stretch.

The sound didn't come again. No chair moving. No music playing. Just that single shift in the wood.

Morgan stayed still for a long time, one hand resting on the book, the other curled around the edge of the blanket.

She didn't feel afraid.

That was the part that surprised her. Even with all the strange little oddities—the music, the smells, the quiet creaking—it hadn't turned to fear. Just awareness. As if someone, or something, was still watching, but not in judgment. Just as witness.

If this had been her Atlanta apartment, she would've blamed it on the upstairs neighbors, on the water pipes, on bad insulation. But here, in the stillness of The Bar, there was nothing to pin it on. No one above, no one below. Just her and the marsh pressing close against the walls.

The fire dimmed.

She stood, stretched, and closed the book with one hand. Left it on the coffee table. Turned out the lamp but let the fire burn down on its own.

She looked out the window into the blackness beyond. Rain tapped softly on the glass.

She walked back through the quiet and settled onto the couch again, blanket pulled tight to her chin, the last edge of warmth tucked under her heels.

The rain stayed steady.

Sleep came slow.

But it came.

Morgan woke to a soft gray light and the sound of the wind moving through the trees—not harsh, not loud, just a low, steady hush like the house was still sleeping.

The fire had gone cold in the night, and the air in the cabin carried that damp, earthy chill that came with rain and early morning.

She didn't get up right away. One hand under her cheek, the other tucked beneath the quilt. There was no rush. Nothing pressing. The world outside her little corner of the marsh would have to spin without her for now.

Eventually, she sat up, pulled on her sweatshirt, and walked barefoot to the kitchen.

"Second verse: same as the first."

She boiled water for coffee and sipped it standing up, watching a single crow work its way across the yard in slow, hopping passes.

Beyond the crow, puddles glimmered in the grass where the rain had pooled. The reeds along the edge of the marsh leaned heavy with water, each drop catching the first threads of light. The smell of the river drifted through the cracked window. A heron lifted out of the shallows, wings beating the mist loose, and for a moment the whole marsh seemed to move in concert.

The house was quiet.

For the first time since arriving, Morgan didn't feel like she was a visitor.

She felt like she lived here.

After breakfast, she opened the hall closet. It stuck a little. The door always stuck at the top, and the bottom edge dragged across the floor.

Inside was the usual mess: an old vacuum, a half-strung box of Christmas lights, a broken folding chair, and a bag of paper napkins with a yellowed plastic fork tucked inside.

Morgan stared at it for a while.

Not because she planned to clean it—not today—but because the whole thing annoyed her. It had always been like this. Too messy to use, too minor to matter. The kind of space everyone ignored.

She shoved the door back into place with her hip and held it there until the latch caught.

"I gotta fix that," she muttered, not for the first time.

But she didn't.

Instead, she walked back into the kitchen, flipped open her notebook, and ran her fingers over the blank page. A breeze passed through the window she'd cracked open earlier, shifting the curtain and brushing gently across her forearm.

She didn't start writing.

But she didn't close the notebook, either.

The rest of the afternoon passed without direction. Morgan began pulling a few nails from the back porch rail that had begun to rust sideways. Nothing urgent. No big project. Just the kind of work that made the house feel tended to.

Around four, the sun broke through—a soft, diffused gold that slipped past the trees and warmed the floor in slow-moving bands. Morgan stood in it for a while, barefoot, letting the light reach her shoulder blades.

She thought about calling someone. Claire, maybe. Just to say hello. Ashley?

But she didn't.

The house was so quiet by then it felt like sound would fracture it. Not in a fragile way—more like cracking the thin ice on the surface of water that had just reached freezing.

She pulled her sweater close, stepped out onto the porch, and sat. One rock. One beer. Just listening.

No creaks. No voices. No music from the far side of the room.

Today it was just her.

CHAPTER 9

The world to be lived in

The sky hung low and cloud-thick, as if the sun had decided to stay tucked in today. Morgan stood at the front window, arms folded, watching wind ripple slowly acrcss the water. The porch screen clicked once in its frame and settled again. No birdsong yet—just the long hush that comes before weather makes up its mind.

She hadn't slept poorly, but she hadn't drifted either. The night had curled in around her, still and wide, and for once, she hadn't fought it.

She noticed the hall closet door had popped open again—just slightly, just enough to catch the corner of her eye. She turned and nudged it closed with her hip, hearing that familiar scrape of wood against floor. The latch didn't catch. Again.

She made a mental note: fix that damn thing.

It wasn't urgent. But it was getting old. Almost a battle of wills. Maybe she would just nail it shut!

She walked back to the kitchen and opened the window an inch, enough to catch the shift in pressure. A low front was coming through—maybe rain, maybe not. The air had that tight, metallic edge to it that said something was near.

By mid-morning, the air had settled into a comfortable warmth—the kind that lingered on her skin without pressing. She tied her hair up and raised a couple of windows, letting the cross breeze move through the rooms in lazy drafts. The roof creaked once in approval. It didn't feel closed in, just soft around the edges.

Morgan had a special project this afternoon. The delivery came just before lunch—a low rumble up the drive, tires crunching over dry gravel. Morgan stepped onto the porch, watching the box truck back in slow beside the pecan tree.

Two young guys hopped out, all grins and careful hands.

"Delivery for Morgan Langford?" one asked.

"That's me."

They carried it in and set it where she pointed—acrcss from the couch, just under the faded old map of South Carolina her granddad used to trace with a pen cap while nervously standing and watching football. The television was a 50-inch and the streaming device came in a separate box.

Morgan signed the tablet and thanked them both.

"This is a great place!", the taller one asked, glancing around the porch. "Did you buy or renting?"

"Neither... my grandad built it a long time ago."

"He knew what he was doing! I can tell it's got good bones."

When they pulled away, she leaned against the doorway for a long second, grinning at the box like it was Christmas.

It had been years since she'd watched a game at The Bar. Time to get to work.

She added a stack of albums onto the console and pressed play. The opening bars of "King of the Road" burst through the speakers—that offhand charm sounded like cracked leather barstools and free matchbooks.

"Trailers for sale or rent…"

Morgan laughed under her breath. Let it play.

There was something about that voice—easy, worn—that set the mood. Not lonely, not even restless. Just… unbothered. Some days unbothered was as good as it got.

She wiped down the counters and sang along to the chorus without thinking. The house had started to echo her again—not with words, not with anything you could name. But in the way old places do when they start remembering who they're holding.

Morgan set the flatscreen up slowly—remote in one hand, peanuts simmering on the stove, the hiss of salt brine mixing with Roger Miller still humming from the record player. She'd picked them up from Truluck's that morning, just as the first roadside stand put out their billboards. She bought a huge bag of green, raw peanuts. First of the season. The small purple-hued peanuts they shipped up from Florida. They were her favorite.

She scooped one from the pot with a slotted spoon, cracking the shell carefully between her teeth. The brine hit first—hot and salty—before the peanut softened into something warm and earthy. She closed her eyes a moment. Granddad used to sit in the same room during summer games, a cold beer sweating beside him, a paper towel pile of peanut shells growing taller with every inning. She could almost hear the faint scrape of his chair when he shifted during a tense at-bat.

Baseball, beer, and salty boiled peanuts.

Some things, she thought, made more sense with age.

Jimmy showed up about an hour later, knocking once before letting himself in.

"Baseball Saturday at the Bar, baby!!"

Morgan turned from the kitchen, grinning. "Oh yeah!"

"Is that new?" he asked, eyeing the setup and nodding toward the flatscreen.

"Isn't it lucky for you that I live so close? You would have to watch this game and eat all those peanuts by yourself." He pulled a fake sad face.

Morgan laughed. "Ok smart ass… sit down and let's see what the Braves have in store for us this season. Heart attack, heart burn or heart break."

They settled in easy—Jimmy with a handful of peanuts that were not quite done, Morgan with a fresh beer. The game was already in the second inning, scoreless, and the announcers were stretching through early-season optimism like it was gospel.

Jimmy nudged her with his elbow. "You still hog the best spot on the couch."

Morgan smirked. "Yeah, well, peanuts. That earns me this seat."

He barked out a laugh. "Fair enough."

By the fourth inning, Jimmy had sent a group text to his brother and sister. Pete and Jenn.

"Braves game at The Bar. Peanuts. BYOB. Morgan's home. Don't be lame."

Morgan caught him typing and raised an eyebrow.

"What'd you do?"

"Nothin'!" he said, grinning. "I'm not the only one who's missed you!"

Sure enough, twenty minutes later, Pete's truck pulled up, followed closely by Jenn's old sedan. They came through the door like they always had—loud, hungry, and full of stories that didn't need context.

"Feels like high school summer in here," Pete said, reaching for the pot of boiled peanuts. "Except better beer. Don't tell Margaret I said that."

Jenn wrapped Morgan in a quick hug, then flopped onto the couch beside her. "Girl, it is good to see you back home!"

For a split second, Morgan saw them all as kids again—Pete lighting M80s on ant hills in the yard, Jenn painting her nails on the porch steps, Jimmy teaching her how to spit sunflower seed shells as far as the pecan tree. The memory blurred into the present, the laughter echoing just the same.

Pleased, Jimmy leaned back, hands behind his head, and nodded toward the porch.

"Aunt Margaret's on the way, too. Said she's bringing dinner."

Morgan blinked, surprised. "She never comes out here."

"All of us here together for the first time in 15 years. You think she's gonna stay away?"

By the time Margaret arrived, the Braves were up by two, and the living room was buzzing with cheers and conversation.

She stepped through the door with a large paper sack in one hand and a familiar smirk on her face. "Well, look at this. I figured if y'all were gonna revive some traditions, the least I could do was halfway cater."

She set the bag on the kitchen counter—pulled pork sandwiches from Moore's BBQ, still warm, wrapped in deliciously greasy wax paper. An extra waxy bag of hushpuppies made this Saturday afternoon as close to perfect as one can get.

Morgan leaned against the doorway, arms folded. "Did Jimmy guilt you into it?"

"No," Margaret said, pulling off her jacket. "I wanted to see you with my own eyes. Making sure you weren't skipping meals."

Morgan gave her a big smile and a strong hug.

Morgan took it all in—the voices overlapping, the chairs pulled close, the clink of bottles, and the occasional burst of laughter when someone remembered a story they hadn't told in years. It wasn't loud, but it was full. A kind of easy chaos that made the place feel used again.

The Bar hadn't felt this kind of life in a long time.

And neither had she.

Margaret wandered down the hallway after refilling her iced tea—half headed for the bathroom, half curious to see what Morgan had been up to.

She paused near the closet.

"Won't stay shut?" she called back over her shoulder.

Morgan glanced up from the couch. "Nope. Latch won't catch. I keep meaning to fix it."

Margaret ran her fingers along the edge of the doorframe.

Morgan stood, walked halfway down the hall. "Probably just warped wood. Or the hinges are off."

Margaret didn't answer. She watched the door creak slightly, as if shifting on its own. And then she nudged it shut again.

By the time the game ended, the living room was half-lit and quiet again. Pete and Jenn had cleared out just after the seventh-inning stretch—things to take care of at home. Jimmy had helped clean up a bit before heading out, and Margaret, true to form, had folded the kitchen towel and left her cup rinsed in the sink.

Morgan stood by the door once she was alone again, looking out across the porch as dusk deepened the trees. The marsh shimmered faintly in the falling light, and the silence returned—not as a vacuum, but as a familiar rhythm. Like breath.

She stepped outside with the last of her beer and sat on the newly repaired steps. They held her without question.

The cabin really felt lived in today. It had been.

She tilted her head back and watched the first stars appear.

The closet down the hall was quiet again, shut, but only barely.

She'd fix the latch.

Eventually.

But not tonight.

She felt full inside—not just from barbecue or beer, but from being surrounded by people whose love for her was as unconditional as it was complete.

She leaned back on her hands and exhaled.

The Bar was feeling alive again. And so was she.

CHAPTER 10

A heavy burden of the past

A few quiet days had passed since the family gathering, and Morgan found herself almost settled. Even a little bit content.

The sun had climbed by the time Morgan made her way out to the utility room. She wasn't looking for anything in particular — just chasing down a stray thought about fire ants. There was a mound by the steps that had sprung up overnight, and she wanted to see if she could find some ant killer.

It hadn't changed much. Grease and gasoline. A stacked-together memory of cut grass and gas cans and rags just clean enough to hold onto. She nudged aside a rusted rake and an old five-gallon bucket with no handle, scanning the shelves that lined the far wall.

Something caught her eye beneath a pile of canvas drop cloths. She tugged them aside—and froze.

Her old tackle box.

It was the small one Granddad had given her when he got himself a new one — blue and plastic, with a faded orange Clemson Football sticker on the side. She hadn't thought about it in years. Hadn't even realized it was still here.

She carried it outside and set it on the porch steps. Sat down next to it and let the light catch the rough edges of her memory.

The latch was a bit rusted, but it opened easily. Inside, the compartments still held a few of her old lures — a chipped red spoon, a rubber worm so dry it cracked in her hand. A tiny container of PowerBait that had turned to chalk. Taped to the underside of the lid was a folded scrap of notebook paper. Her name, in childhood scrawl: "Morgan's Property."

She smiled at that. The handwriting was pressed too hard, almost gouging the paper in places — the way kids write when they really mean something. She remembered Granddad chuckling at it, tapping the sticker with his thumb, and saying, "Well now it's official. Nobody can argue with the Tigers and a no trespassing sign."

But the smile flickered and faded just as fast. The last time she had opened it was the final time she and Granddad fished together. She could still see his hands cutting bait, the smell of damp worms on the porch rail, the sound of him spitting into the water for luck — "Old sailor's trick," he told her. She'd believed him for years. She remembered him saying when she was a little older he was going to buy her a nicer rod and reel. She had almost outgrown the little Zebco handed down from Pete.

Morgan closed the lid and went back to her day. Cleaned up the shed a little, raked out the corners. Tried to stay busy. But the box followed her, somehow. Sat there in her thoughts even when she turned on music or got the washer going.

She made it through the morning, but everything felt distant. Like she was piloting her body from a few feet away. She did the dishes. Took a shower. Stared at the tackle box again. But the silence wasn't comforting today. It pressed in from all sides.

By early afternoon, she pulled on clean jeans, grabbed her keys, and drove into town.

At the store, she didn't hesitate. Walked past the bread and milk. She stood there for a moment, eyeing the rows — then picked up a bottle of Jim Beam. Not out of ceremony or shame. Just a quiet, resigned kind of need to quiet her mind.

She didn't speak to anyone when she checked out.

That night, Morgan had a fitful sleep.

She'd thought the bourbon would help, but instead it turned her brain loose. She tossed for hours, hot and then cold, covers kicked to the floor. No real dreams. Just scraps.

When she did finally fall under, it was thick and slow, like sinking into the bottom of a warm lake.

She woke just after 3am, not all at once but in aching pieces. Her mouth dry. Her shoulder pressed into the couch seam. One foot bare, the other still in a sock. A long, sour taste at the back of her throat that wasn't quite regret but was in the neighborhood.

It took a minute to remember the voice.

Not a dream. Or if it was, it had cracked through from just below the surface. She could still feel the echo of it, low and calm, not unkind. Almost the feeling of breath on her ear.

"You're doin' fine, kid."

Everything was still. Except for that part of her, way down, that was suddenly not.

Her breath caught sharp in her throat, a sudden chill rising along her arms. She almost whispered back without meaning to — the instinct felt that natural. But no words came.

She sat up quickly and looked around the room — the familiar half-cluttered warmth of it — and felt the weight of something invisible. Not menacing. Just... present.

Her thoughts tried to form an explanation. Whiskey dream. Residual sound from a record. A memory of her grandfather's voice, muddled and misremembered.

But the cadence hadn't been Granddad's.

This was rougher, steadier, without the slur of whiskey but with the gravel of age. A stranger's voice that somehow felt like it had always known her.

She got up and made her way into the kitchen for water. Drank from the faucet. Wiped her mouth with the sleeve of her sweatshirt. The taste of last night lingered — smoky and bitter — and she couldn't quite shake it. Not the sound of those words, either. The way they landed. Comforting and gentle.

She moved through the house without turning on lights, as if someone else might still be sleeping.

Later, after the sun was up and the morning made everything feel more ordinary, she'd tell herself she imagined it. That she'd been drunk, exhausted, maybe even dreaming. She'd file it away somewhere between wishful thinking and an old floorboard creaking.

But for now, in the dark hush of early morning, she sat on the edge of the couch, elbows on knees, and just listened. Only silence. Still and full.

She poured another drink, swallowed it fast, and sank back into the couch.

Morgan woke late, the light already sharp at the windows. Her head thudded with that dull, post-whiskey rhythm — not a full hangover, just enough to slow her down. Her mouth was dry, her skin tight with sweat, and the taste of char clung to her tongue.

She didn't move right away. Just lay there on the couch, one arm over her eyes, trying to piece the night back together.

The records. The porch. The bottle.

And then the voice.

"You're doin' fine, kid."

She sat up slowly, blinking hard, her stomach unsettled. The coffee might help, she told herself, though she didn't quite feel like she deserved any comfort just yet. The bottle still sat on the floor by the couch where she'd left it. Only a third gone, but that was enough.

She moved barefoot to the cold tile. Her body ached in strange places, like it always did when emotions hit you with a square punch.

She needed to talk to someone who remembered him the way she did. Someone who wouldn't treat it like a problem to solve.

So she picked up her phone and called Jimmy.

He answered on the second ring with his usual mock suspicion: "Morgan Langford. Calling before noon? What's wrong, Bar on fire?"

She laughed, but it caught a little. "Can you come by?"

There was a pause, then, softer: "Yeah. Of course. You all right?"

"I don't know," she said. "I think I just want to sit on the porch and not be alone."

"I'll be there in twenty. You want me to bring anything?"

She looked at the counter. "Hangover breakfast. And something cold."

"Say less."

She hung up, stared at the phone for a second longer than necessary, then set it down. The house felt a bit lighter already.   He pulled up just after ten, tires crunching softly over the sand. She met him halfway down the walk, barefoot and still in the same sweatshirt from last night. He stepped out holding a grease-stained paper sack and glass-bottle Cokes, dripping with condensation.

"I come bearing gifts, ye old drunk!" he said, lifting the bag like it held the crown jewels. "Hot, greasy, and guaranteed to cure whatever kind of self-inflicted suffering you've got brewing."

She smiled, genuine this time. "You're a damn saint."

They sat on the porch steps like they were kids again. The sausage biscuits were wrapped in white paper, still steaming. Jimmy handed her a Coke and cracked his open with a hiss.

"Looks better out here than I remember," he said, glancing at the cleared yard, the trimmed porch, the now-functional step. "You've been busy."

"I needed the motion," she said. "Still do."

He nodded, then bit into his biscuit and chewed thoughtfully. "So," he said, mouth half-full, "you gonna tell me what this is about, or do I just sit here and keep complimenting your grass mowing?"

She took a drink first. Cold, sharp. "I heard something last night."

He didn't say anything. Just waited.

"Not like a sound. A voice. Just one line." She paused. "You're doin' fine, kid. That's it."

He studied her a second. "Like Granddad?"

She shook her head. "It wasn't him. I don't know how I know that — I just do. It was something else, but it felt close to my ear."

Jimmy let that settle. "What have you been drinking?"

"Just JB."

"Enough to hear things?"

She looked at him, steady. "Maybe. But it didn't feel like something I made up."

He nodded again, slower this time. He didn't rush a joke, which told her he was taking her seriously in a way Jimmy rarely let show. Then finally, his grin broke through. "Well," he said finally, "you always did have an open line to the weird."

She laughed, then leaned into him a little. "Thanks for not calling me crazy."

"I didn't say you weren't crazy. I just said it's nothing new."

She let out a breath that almost felt like relief. They sat in silence for a few minutes, watching a pair of cardinals flit between the trees. The wind had picked up just enough to make the palmettos rustle softly as if they were sharing a secret.

Jimmy crushed his empty biscuit wrapper into the paper bag. "You know, he talked about you all the time," he said. "Like—constantly. I think half the guys at the dock knew you were going to be the next Harper Lee."

She didn't answer right away. Just traced her finger along the edge of the porch step.

"That's what makes it worse," she said finally, her voice low. "If I mattered that much, how could he just go without saying goodbye?"

Jimmy looked at her. There wasn't anything easy to offer in return.

"I was ten," she said. "Just a kid. And one day he was there, and the next day he was a funeral no one would explain."

He stayed quiet. Let her speak.

"I've spent years trying to be okay with it. Telling myself he must've been hurting in some way I couldn't see. But it doesn't add up. He wasn't sick. He didn't leave a note. Nothing."

She drew in a shaky breath, let it out slow. "I keep thinking about that last morning. I don't even remember if I hugged him."

Jimmy reached over and squeezed her knee. "You were a kid. He knew you loved him."

"But did he know I needed him?" she said.

That part came out smaller than she meant it to.

Jimmy didn't offer any answer, just stayed there beside her. Steady as ever.

Jimmy stayed quiet a long time. Long enough for the wind to pass through the pines again and for

Morgan to wonder if she'd said too much. Then he leaned back on his hands and looked out over the marsh.

"You remember when we used to sneak into his truck cab and pretend it was a spaceship?"

She blinked. "What?"

"You were maybe seven. I was nine. He'd park it in the shade behind the house and we'd climb in and sit there making Space Shuttle noises. You put that plastic strainer on your head like it was a helmet." Morgan laughed at the visual.

She gave him a look. "That was my command module."

"Right. And you wouldn't let me drive."

"I was the pilot. I wouldn't let you fly. You were a mission specialist so you didn't get to pilot too."

He grinned. "Point is, he caught us one day and instead of getting mad, he tossed us each a MoonPie and told us to 'aim for the stars but try not to dent the fender.'"

She smiled, despite herself. "I forgot about that."

"Yeah, well," Jimmy said, glancing over at her. "He didn't. He brought it up a couple years later when I talked about learning to drive. Said, 'Reach for the stars, but don't dent the fender.' That's how his mind worked. Quiet, weird, perfect."

They sat with that for a beat.

"I guess what I'm trying to say," Jimmy went on, "is you meant everything to him. And I hate what happened. I hate what he did. But it wasn't about you."

Morgan nodded, eyes shining. "I know."

But in the quiet after his words, she realized she didn't fully believe it yet. Not in her bones. That was the part still waiting for her.

He nudged her with his elbow and flashed his biggest smile.

Jimmy stayed for another hour, long enough for a second Coke and some talk about baseball and whatever Pete's youngest had crashed the golf cart into that week.

He didn't press, didn't circle back to the heavy stuff. Just let it hang between them like something sacred, not meant to be dissected.

When he finally stood to go, he paused at the bottom of the steps and looked back at her.

"You call me, okay? Even if you don't know what to say."

Morgan nodded. "I will. Thanks Jim."

He gave her a quick salute and walked to his truck, the gravel crunching behind him like punctuation. He lingered at the door longer than he needed to, one hand on the frame, as if half-expecting her to call him back. When she didn't, he just gave her another grin and disappeared into the trees.

She watched him go, the tailgate glinting as he turned back toward the road.

After he disappeared down the curve, Morgan sat for a while longer. The porch was warm in the sun, but the breeze still carried an edge. She pulled her knees up to her chest and rested her chin there, letting the quiet fold around her.

No music. No whiskey. No ghosts. Just the creak of the swing and the soft, distant call of a mourning dove.

She didn't feel better, exactly. But she didn't feel alone.

When the shadows started to stretch long across the yard, she finally stood and went inside. Dishes still in the sink. Laundry still in the dryer. Life, still moving forward in small ways.

She grabbed the bottle of Jim Beam, ran her thumb across the label and put it away in the cabinet above the fridge.

It was time to open up the bedroom.

It's not a shrine. And that damn couch sucks.

Morgan walked down the hall with purpose. She wedged the door open with her foot and opened both windows wide, letting the light and salt air flood in. Dust lifted in little spirals, curtains ballooned softly, and the bedspread — still his, still tucked tight — released the faintest trace of cedar and age. For the first time since she'd come home, it didn't feel like absence

CHAPTER 11

Worn the way rooms get worn

His bedroom didn't hit as hard as she expected.

Morgan stood in the doorway, arms crossed, waiting for the gut punch that never came. It looked more like a guest room than a museum — neutral, quiet, a little stale but definitely not sad or haunted. Of course, Margaret cleaned it out years ago.

The bed was made, the quilt neatly folded. His highback leather chair and antique floor lamp sat by the window, angled and still ready to be used for reading. The dresser drawers were empty. The closet held nothing but a few wire hangers and an old ironing board — once she managed to get it open.

She let out a breath she hadn't realized she'd been holding.

The room wasn't a shrine. It was just a room with a double bed her back could really use.

Morgan stripped the bed, tossed the linens into the wash, and dusted every surface — even the closet.

She paused once while dusting the dresser, remembering how as a child she used to tiptoe past this very doorway at night. Back then the room had smelled faintly of English Leather and old books. Sometimes she'd hear Granddad's low snore, steady as the marsh tide, or the creak of this same leather chair as he shifted his weight. She'd hurry past quickly, not wanting to be caught awake after bedtime — but secretly comforted by knowing he was there.

She went back to the front room, grabbed the duffel she'd been living out of, and started making trips. Clothes in the drawers, jeans hung on the closet bar. A handful of books stacked on the nightstand. A pair of sandals kicked under the bed.

It didn't feel odd or intrusive to fill the space with her things. A sweatshirt folded into the drawer. A hair tie left on the nightstand. By the fifth trip she realized the room was beginning to carry her scent — soap, paper, coffee — instead of just dust.

Sunlight through the bedroom windows made the hallway feel warmer — like the house was smiling at the change. By mid-morning the washing machine hummed and Morgan had a sense she could only describe as calm.

She stood in the middle of the room with her hands on her hips, taking stock.

Not bad. Not just Granddad's anymore. But not quite hers alone.

She showered, changed into fresh clothes and brought the damp quilt outside to hang for a little while over the porch rail, just to let it breathe. The sun was warm enough now to feel like April had taken over.

Back inside, she opened one of the windows a little wider and started stacking a few books on the shelf near the dresser — a mix of her own and some that had been scattered through the house. A Hemingway, of course.

A battered paperback copy of *Their Eyes Were Watching God* she hadn't realized she'd brought. A short story collection — the receipt tucked inside as a makeshift bookmark.

As she shifted a couple of volumes to make room, something slipped — not loudly, just enough to catch her attention.

A thin, square object wedged between the last row of books. It had ended up on the floor all the way at the bottom of the shelves.

She reached back and pulled it out gently. The moment her fingertips touched it, she could tell it was brittle with age.

A photograph.

Old, black and white. Granddad, younger than she'd ever seen him — maybe in his twenties — with three other men, all in short sleeves and sunglasses, standing on the bow of a docked boat with palm trees and an old Chevy Bel Air in the background.

On the back, written in pencil, just: Havana '60.

She sat down on the edge of the bed and looked at it for a long time.

The sharp contrast of the photograph drew her in. She studied the set of his shoulders, the faint grin barely lifting his face, and wondered who had taken it. Had he been carefree then? Or restless? She imagined the humid air, the heavy music of Spanish voices rising from the street, the clink of glass bottles somewhere just out of frame.

It unsettled her in a way she couldn't name. She had always pictured Granddad as firmly rooted to this stretch of South Carolina, bound to the tides and tides alone. But here he was, on a boat in Havana, looking younger, lighter, maybe freer. A whole other story she hadn't known existed.

She was going to have to ask Margaret about this one.

She slid the photo into the drawer of the nightstand, careful not to bend it.

She'd remember to ask her the next time they were together.

Back on the porch, the quilt had dried into a soft sun-warmed weight. She pulled it from the railing, gave it a shake, and brought it back inside.

The fabric smelled of grass and clean air, and when she carried it through the hall, she thought of Margaret beating rugs over the porch rail in summer. She'd been six or seven, sitting cross-legged with a glass of sweet tea, watching the dust rise like ghosts. Those little domestic rituals — quilts, laundry, dishes — had held the house together more than she realized.

The bedroom smelled fresher now. She made the bed with practiced hands, smoothing the corners, fluffing the pillows.

It was the first time she'd properly made a bed in months. She was actually looking forward to bedtime.

Morgan took a step back and looked at it — not the way you admire a photo in a magazine, but something you were happy with nonetheless.

The house was quiet again — in the best kind of way.

She spent the next hour finishing small things.

Wiping down baseboards. Folding the laundry. Replacing the dead bulb in the closet.

Each act, however ordinary, felt like laying claim. The scrape of her sponge against the baseboard, the snap of a drawer shutting, the warm hum of the dryer — all of it stitched her life a little more tightly into the fabric of The Bar.

There was comfort in the simplicity of it — the mundane kind of comfort that came from knowing exactly what to do with your hands.

She brewed a fresh pot of coffee and carried it back to the bedroom in her favorite chipped mug. Sat for a minute in the leather chair by the window, listening to the breeze tick through the palmettos and the buzz of a boat engine way out past the marsh.

The photograph stayed in the drawer, untouched, but it didn't weigh the room down.

If anything, it made the air feel richer — like the walls had stories of their own and were finally willing to share them. In time.

The floor creaked once in the hallway.

She looked up, just slightly.

Morgan sipped her coffee and let the sound pass through her, like wind through reeds.

By late afternoon, the bedroom felt like part of the house again. Not hidden.

Morgan folded the last of her clothes — a stack of soft T-shirts, most of them faded from years of wear — and slid the drawer shut with her hip.

She looked around once more. Nothing fancy. But it was hers now.

For the first time, she didn't feel like she was borrowing space from the past. The room answered back differently — not with memory, not with grief, but with something closer to welcome.

She wandered out to the porch and stood there a moment, letting the sun warm her shoulders. A few gulls wheeled overhead. Down by the far edge of the yard, a lizard darted across the brick walkway and disappeared under the azaleas.

No revelations. Just light, movement, and air.

Back inside, she jotted a quick note on the back of a grocery receipt: Ask Margaret about Havana.

She stuck it on the fridge with a magnet shaped like a banana — one of the old ones that had been there since she was little.

She made herself a simple dinner — a tomato sandwich, kettle chips straight from the bag, and half a beer she hadn't finished.

On the record player, Patsy Cline's "Walkin' After Midnight" slipped through the room, low and steady.

The bedroom was ready now, but she didn't go back there just yet.

She sat on the couch with her legs tucked under her, a book in her lap, the breeze drifting in through the open windows.

A soft clink from the hallway. Probably the closet again. She didn't check.

The song ended, and the silence that followed didn't feel like something missing.

It felt like it belonged to her.

And she belonged to The Bar. That was fine.

CHAPTER 12

When we are at our best

Morgan woke early, blinking up at the ceiling. For a split second, her mind caught on the question of where she was.

Then she smiled.

The bedroom was quiet in the soft gray light. No creaks, no footsteps, no ghostly sighs — just the deep, even stillness of a place that felt like home now.

She pulled on jeans and a hoodie, walked barefoot down the hall, and started hot water for coffee.

While it heated, she stepped out onto the porch. The air was cooler than she expected — sharp enough to wake her up fully, but not unfriendly. Down by the trees, mist hovered over the marsh, rising like breath from the earth.

A cardinal flashed across the yard, then disappeared into the brush. She smiled without thinking. Cardinals had meaning. Margaret always said so.

Back inside, she poured her coffee, sat at the kitchen table, and opened her notebook.

Not to write. Not yet. Just to see.

A few words stared back at her from the previous day:

Don't force it. Just listen.

She closed the cover and turned the page in her mind instead.

She didn't bother making a list that morning.

The to-dos would find her on their own.

Maybe the sticky drawer in the kitchen — the one that always stuck halfway and had to be jiggled just right.

Maybe the shutter on the back bedroom window — the one that had been banging in the wind two nights ago. Three turns of the wrench, and it would hold steady.

The work wasn't urgent.

She moved through the house slowly, not cleaning so much as tending. Picking up, straightening, noticing what had been left crooked or half-finished.

In the front hall, she passed the closet and paused.

The door was ajar again. Just slightly.

She nudged it shut without stopping.

By noon, she was dusty, a little sweaty, and feeling more grounded than she had in days. She opened windows wide, turned on the ceiling fans, and let the breeze move through the rooms like a rinse.

She made herself a sandwich — egg salad with too much pepper, a handful of chips, and a sweet tea poured over half-melted ice. She ate it on the porch, bare feet propped on the rail, watching the marsh breathe under the warming sky.

The breeze had picked up — not cool anymore, just steady.

The kind that said April was settling in for good.

Somewhere down the road, a truck rumbled past and stirred the dust. A dog barked in answer. Morgan didn't move.

The photo from the bedroom was still on her mind — Havana, 1960. Granddad looking young and unfamiliar.

She hadn't asked Margaret about it yet. Not over the phone. She wanted to share the photo with her.

She tried to picture it: her grandfather, not the man she remembered in boots and work shirts, but one who wore sunglasses and grinned on a dock in Cuba. What was he doing there? Fishing? Drinking? Maybe both. The Havana she imagined was hot, crowded, and loud — tobacco smoke, steel guitars, the clatter of dice in an alley. It was hard to reconcile with the man who whittled branches into fishing poles for her on summer afternoons. But there was more to him. Maybe there always had been.

Inside, the house had taken on that familiar, late-afternoon hush — warm walls, creaking floors, quiet corners.

She finished the last of her tea and went back in, not to work, not to rest, just to be there.

She wandered into the bedroom and stood for a minute in the middle of the floor, not sure what had drawn her back in.

The bed was neatly made, the window still cracked open, letting in the hush of the trees.

She ran a hand across the top of the dresser. Nothing to straighten. Nothing to fix.

No next thing.

So she sat.

The high back leather chair by the window creaked as she settled in. She tucked her legs under her, opened the Hemingway she'd brought from the living room, and started to read.

She didn't make it far. The words blurred after a few pages, not from tiredness, but from something softer — a kind of stillness.

It reminded her of Ashley — the way she used to blur Morgan's edges, too. One memory rose, uninvited: a Saturday in high school, the two of them on the bleachers during a preseason game. Neither cared about the score. Ashley had stretched out in the sun, her laugh louder than the crowd, her hair sticking to her cheek from the heat. Morgan had pretended to watch the field but memorized that exact shade of light on her instead. She still carried it. Some memories lived like that — tucked in a pocket, worn smooth by the years, impossible to lose. From the stack she'd loaded, a record finished with a low click and shifted to another.

Then came the crackle of vinyl, followed by a voice as rough and holy as the dust — Ray Charles, singing about Spanish angels and unspoken prayers.

She closed the book, let it rest on her chest, and leaned her head back.

The house wrapped its arms around her.

Even the quiet had a texture now. She could smell the faint sweetness of the wood, warmed by sun and salt air. The floors radiated a soft heat under her bare feet, and the breeze through the screen carried the sharp tang of the marsh, tidal and alive. It was the kind of stillness that just gave itself, piece by piece, until she felt steadier without realizing it.

When the song ended, she didn't get up right away.

There was no whisper from the hallway, no faint smell of smoke. Just the soft tick of the cooling record and the steady breath of the breeze through the screen.

Eventually, she stood, stretched, and walked the quiet length of the hallway — passing the closet without looking at it.

In the kitchen, she popped open a cold beer. A squirrel darted along the fence line. A crow cawed overhead.

154

That didn't feel like a failure. It felt like freedom.

CHAPTER 13

In the shade of the old days

By mid-morning the next day, the air already felt different—heavier.

Still spring, but the kind that whispered of the heat to come.

Morgan stood barefoot in the kitchen, sipping her second cup of coffee, window cracked just enough to let the breeze stir the edge of the curtain. She could hear something out back—maybe squirrels on the roof, or branches shifting in the wind.

She'd slept well.

Not the fogged-over crash of exhaustion—the real kind. The way a kid sleeps.

The light in the kitchen had that pale-gold look that never lasts more than half an hour—the moment between morning and day. The marsh smell drifted in, cool and faintly metallic, like wet clay. She ran a finger along the rim of her mug, tracing the chip she'd never quite managed to smooth away.

She rinsed her cup, set it upside down in the rack, and opened the back door.

Sunlight spread across the steps like a welcome. She stepped out and blinked into the brightness.

Somewhere in the distance, a screen door slammed—not hers. Maybe one of the closer neighbors.

Morgan didn't feel restless. But she felt... ready.

For what, she wasn't sure.

She went back inside and leaned against the counter, letting her hands warm on the ceramic mug. The photo was still in the drawer of the nightstand.

She'd looked at it twice since finding it, both times with the same quiet unease. Not fear. Just questions.

Morgan pulled out her phone and stared at it for a second before tapping Margaret's name. It only rang once.

"Hey, sweetheart," Margaret answered. "Everything alright?"

"Yeah," Morgan said. "I just—do you have plans tonight? I was thinking about making something. Maybe grill? If you want to come by."

There was a pause. Not long. Just the kind that meant something else was being considered.

"I'd love to," Margaret said. "Want me to bring anything?"

"Just your sweet self," Morgan said.

Another pause. "Alright. I'll be there around five."

They said their goodbyes, and when Morgan set the phone down, she let her hand rest on the counter a moment longer. Not because she was nervous. Just because it felt good to know someone was coming.

She looked out the window, the water still rippling in slow-motion waves. A white heron glided past the far edge of the water and vanished behind the pines. For a second, she thought of Atlanta—of her apartment, the steady buzz—and felt no pull to go back. The quiet here wasn't emptiness anymore. It was company.

The hours drifted easy—the kind that slipped through her hands without her noticing, the sort of day that didn't need to prove itself.

Morgan spent the next hour cleaning the top of the old brick grill that Granddad built in the side yard. He'd built it to last—two large grilling surfaces at different heights, and a heavy hood made for smoking pork. As she scrubbed, the memories came easy—barbecue chicken, pig pickins, burgers, steaks, oysters.

She could almost smell it now—the mix of charcoal, beer, and brine. Granddad used to tune his old transistor radio to whatever ball game was on, balancing it on the brick ledge while someone handed him a plate through the window. The same radio was still tucked in a box in the utility room. She made a note to find batteries for it later.

Later, she stopped by Truluck's—grabbed a small bag of charcoal, a bottle of lighter fluid, fresh shrimp that had been delivered just off the boat that morning, and whatever vegetables looked good. Zucchini, red onion, bell pepper. She had found a handful of metal skewers in a drawer near the stove.

It felt good to plan something, even something small. To be able to say I'm making dinner and look forward to it.

The house had been patient with her. Maybe it was time to let a little more life in.

Back at The Bar, Morgan cleaned the shrimp, threaded them onto skewers with chunks of vegetables, drizzled everything with olive oil, and hit it with salt, pepper, and a squeeze of lemon.

She worked without rushing—confident, focused.

She didn't cook fancy, but she cooked well. The kind of meals that came together from what you had, made better by heat and time and knowing when to leave it alone.

The grill was hot now, the coals even and white around the edges. She brushed the grate clean one last time and closed the lid to let it build just a little more heat.

Then, almost as an afterthought, she went to the bedroom and opened the nightstand drawer.

Havana, 1960.

She held it by the corners and set it gently on the kitchen counter.

Up close, she noticed new things—the way sunlight fell across the boat deck, a blurred hand at the corner of the frame that must have belonged to the photographer. The image looked alive in the afternoon light, as if ready to tell her a story it hadn't yet decided how to relay.

She wondered what the air had smelled like that day—rum, salt, diesel—and whether he'd laughed the way he used to when the tide came in just right. For the first time, she wished she could have asked him about it.

The gravel crackled under tires just before five.

Morgan looked up from the grill and wiped her hands on a towel.

Margaret stepped out of her car, waving casually like she'd been coming by every week for years. She wore jeans, flip-flops, and a straw hat that looked like it had lived in the back seat most of its life.

"Something smells good," she said as she walked up the steps.

"Grilled shrimp and veggies," Morgan said. "Hope you're hungry."

"Always," Margaret smiled, then nodded toward the grill. "You got that old thing cleaned up nice!"

Morgan grinned. "Yep. Can't beat it."

They sat out on the porch while the skewers cooked—nothing fancy, just the two of them with iced tea, watching the light shift across the marsh. Morgan flipped the shrimp once, checked the heat with the back of her hand. Margaret watched her with something like quiet approval, though she didn't say it.

"You always were good in the kitchen," she said eventually.

"Learned from the best," Morgan replied, not looking up.

"These stairs look much better. You did a nice job on them."

"Oh by the way, I didn't want to mention it when everyone was here the other day," said Morgan. "Thanks for not telling me Ashley runs the hardware store. A little heads-up would've been nice."

Margaret smirked. "Well, you can also thank me for not letting the yard guy fix them —figured you'd have to visit the only place that sells lumber within fifty miles."

Morgan shook her head, laughing. "Always two steps ahead."

"That's my job, honey." Margaret took a sip of tea, ice clicking against the glass. "Some people need a nudge; you needed a project."

"And apparently a reunion," Morgan said.

"Apparently."

They shared the kind of silence that isn't awkward—the kind that means both people are thinking the same thing.

They ate at the small table by the front windows, plates on woven placemats, conversation easy and slow. No big stories, no digging. Just the kind of talk that fills the space without trying.

It wasn't until they were clearing the dishes that Morgan said, "I found something. Wanted to ask you about it."

Margaret raised an eyebrow. "Oh?"

Morgan grabbed the photo and held it out across the table.

Margaret took it gently, turned it in her hands.

"I'll be damned," she said softly. "That's Dad alright. He was so young."

Morgan sat down. "Havana. 1960. You ever hear about that trip?"

Margaret looked at the photo again, thoughtful now. "Eh, bits and pieces. I always figured it was a fishing thing. He didn't talk about it much."

She passed the photo back.

Morgan shrugged, looking down at it. "Just curious."

Margaret nodded. "Well… it was 1960. That must've been before Castro, or right as things started changing. People used to go all the time back then. Fishing, drinking, dancing. He must have had the time of his life."

Morgan traced the corner of the photo with her thumb. "I wonder if he saw Hemingway's home while he was there."

Margaret paused, then smiled. "Now that brings back a memory. I remember Daddy saying Hemingway had already left by then, but the house was still there—filled with his things, like he'd just stepped out for a walk. Dad met one of the caretakers, I think. Had a drink with him."

Morgan pictured it—the clatter of glasses, the hum of a fan, her granddad's rough laugh rising over the sound of a trumpet somewhere down the street. She could almost see him there, younger, unburdened.

Morgan looked up, surprised. "He never told me."

"Well," Margaret said with a soft laugh. "By the time you came along, he had moved on to things closer to home."

Morgan studied the photo one last time. "Funny," she said. "All those years I thought he never left the county."

"He left plenty," Margaret said. "Always came back home."

Morgan smiled at that, the kind of smile that reaches the eyes slowly.

They cleared the dishes together, neither of them in a rush. It reminded Morgan of childhood dinners—the quiet scrape of plates, the clink of silverware, and how Margaret always knew what came next. Back then, she thought that meant Margaret had all the answers. Now, she knew it was something gentler—just presence.

Margaret dried the last glass and set it on the counter. "You've done something good here," she said, looking around. "The place feels... calm. And so do you."

Morgan nodded. "It's getting there," she said. Then, with a half-smile: "Definitely needs a dishwasher if I'm gonna be cooking again."

Margaret laughed. "Well, it survived this long without one."

Morgan shrugged. "Yeah... well I didn't."

Margaret let out a full, head-thrown-back kind of laugh—the contagious kind that made its way over to Morgan.

They stood together for a while afterward, neither speaking. Out beyond the windows, dusk softened the trees into silhouettes, and the first frogs began to call. The porch light hummed faintly against the dark.

Morgan thought, not for the first time, how rare it was to feel both rooted and new.

When Margaret finally hugged her goodnight, she held on an extra beat.

"Get good sleep tonight, now," she said.

Morgan smiled. "I will. You too."

After the car pulled away, The Bar felt quiet again—but not empty. The scent of grilled shrimp and lemon still lingered in the air, the kind of smell that stays on your skin and reminds you you've been cared for and you've cared for someone.

She stood for a moment in the doorway, breathing in the salt and smoke, and thought that maybe this was what peace smelled like.

CHAPTER 14

I had never felt so peaceful

Morgan lingered outside until the shadows shifted and the porch started to cool again. The swing creaked beneath her as she rocked gently, not thinking about much at all — just the hum of evening settling in. When the breeze cooled enough to raise goosebumps, she slipped back inside.

The light inside the cabin had started to turn gold. She flipped on a lamp in the living room and watched it soften the corners of the space — warm against the wood-paneled walls, catching the edges of the books she'd stacked along the shelves.

The air still smelled faintly of grilled shrimp and lemon, that quiet sweetness that lingers after a good night spent — something lived-in, something earned. She stood a moment in the doorway, tracing the outline of light on the floorboards, feeling like she'd crossed into a gentler version of herself.

She found herself reaching for her phone again, thumbing through old texts without really meaning to. A string of unread news alerts. A promotional email from a travel site she hadn't visited in over a year. Claire's name near the top.

She scrolled, paused on an old photo. Her apartment. Atlanta. A pic she'd forgotten — her hair pulled up, takeout on the counter, typed pages spread across the floor.

She didn't feel sad looking at it. Just... finished. Like something had closed and nothing needed to be salvaged.

It wasn't loss anymore, she realized — just space. The kind that makes room for something new before you knew what the future had in store.

She smiled, set the phone down, and went to the kitchen. Started thinking about what she might make tomorrow.

Dinner didn't really need planning. She'd make something simple. Maybe roast the vegetables from the last Truluck's run — squash, bell pepper, sweet onion — and toss them with rice and herbs. Maybe grill again soon if the weather held.

The simple act of deciding felt good — not like duty, but rhythm. The kind her days used to have before deadlines and headlines.

The evening moved easily, without a clock. She lit a few candles and cracked one of the front windows to let in the cooling air. Nighttime AC wasn't far off now.

The record player sat silent. She let it be. Some silences didn't need filling.

Instead, she curled into the corner of the couch with a blanket tossed over her knees and flipped through a few pages of *The Old Man and the Sea*, stopping here and there to reread a sentence. She wasn't looking for anything — just settling into the language again. Letting the rhythm hold her.

She thought of her grandfather's hands, how he used to turn the pages of his books slow, steady, like it mattered that the words got their full weight before being left behind. She tried to read that way now — as if every sentence deserved patience.

Eventually, her eyes grew heavy. She closed the book, left it on the armrest, and walked down the hall to brush her teeth.

The bedroom was cool and quiet. The quilt had kept its scent from the porch line-dry, and the sheets were soft from years of washings. It felt good to lie down and spread out.

She turned onto her side, pressing her face into the pillow — and paused.

Lavender.

Not strong — just a trace. But unmistakable.

She hadn't used anything scented. No fabric softener. No detergent like that in the house.

She opened her eyes, blinking into the low light. The scent was too fresh to be imagined. Too gentle to be threatening. Like someone had misted her pillow.

For a moment, she thought of Margaret — maybe she'd used lavender on the quilt once, long ago, and the scent had risen again under the heat of the day. But something in her gut said no. This was new. This was for her.

Somewhere down the hall, one of the floors gave a small creak.

She didn't sit up.

Didn't call out.

Morgan closed her eyes and drifted.

The morning brought no dreams she could remember. Just the warm weight of the quilt, the pale shift of light behind the curtains, and a quiet that felt a bit expectant.

Morgan stretched, blinked at the ceiling, then rolled to sit on the edge of the bed. The lavender was gone. Or at least she couldn't smell it anymore. Only the familiar, clean scent of air and cotton.

She padded barefoot into the kitchen and started the coffee, reaching for the jar of peanut butter while it brewed. She smeared some on a piece of toast and ate it standing by the sink, watching a squirrel navigate the porch rail like a gymnast on a balance beam.

Her thoughts drifted to the photo again. Havana, 1960. Granddad standing in the sun beside a boat, grinning like a man who had stories to tell and years to tell them.

She tried to picture the version of him that existed before her — younger, louder, maybe even reckless. It was strange to imagine that kind of freedom belonging to him.

She let her mind wander there — to Hemingway's house, before it was a museum, while the air still smelled like smoke and sea salt and the space was sacred.

Walking the tile floors. Peering into the study where the books were still lined on the shelves.

Maybe he ran a hand over the typewriter.

Maybe he didn't even touch a thing — just stood in the doorway, awed.

And later, the bar. Maybe the Floridita. She had heard that name before.

That caretaker in the sharp white shirt, full of stories. The two of them laughing over rum, talking about writing, or fishing, or God knows what.

Morgan smiled into her coffee.

It explained something. Maybe not everything. But enough.

There was a courage in it — the idea of going somewhere alone, seeing something new, carrying it home quietly like a secret souvenir. Maybe she'd inherited that part of him after all.

In the living room, the record player sat still. She thought about putting on something soft — maybe jazz — but decided against it.

Instead, she stepped onto the porch. The swing rocked easily when she settled into it, like it had been waiting for her to wake up.

No footsteps. Nothing creaking.

Just her.

She didn't need the silence to carry everything.

Back inside, she opened her phone and searched for something specific — not a playlist, not an old favorite. Just a sound she wanted to hear. She grabbed her small speaker from the shelf, typed in Buena Vista Social Club, and let the first track play.

The music filled the house gently — soft horns, low strings, a voice worn smooth by time. It sounded like sunshine and cigar smoke, like salt air and rum and stories told in doorways. Like Havana, the way she imagined it.

She didn't know the words.

Didn't need to.

She moved slowly through the kitchen, pouring the last of her coffee and rinsing out the pot. She leaned against the counter as the next song began — slower, sadder. Her body swayed without thinking.

Granddad must've loved it there.

She could see him in it now — easy in his skin, glass in hand, soaking it in like he knew he'd never be back.

The thought didn't make her sad — it made her proud. That he'd lived wide enough to leave a piece of himself somewhere she'd only dreamt of.

Morgan let the music play and it drifted into the corners of the house. Into the hallway. Into the quiet.

The song faded, but she didn't change it. Turned the volume down a bit and let it be her soundtrack for the day.

She returned to the porch swing and pulled the quilt across her lap, even though the day was already warming. Not out of cold. Just comfort.

The water shimmered in the sunlight, soft greens deepening toward gold. Out near the edge, a pair of egrets moved through the reeds like ghosts in slow motion.

Morgan sipped and leaned back. Her body had grown used to this new speed, but her mind was still catching up. There were days it still wanted to race ahead, to solve everything at once.

But maybe that was the lesson — that healing didn't always come with grand revelations. Sometimes it was just sitting still long enough to realize you'd stopped waiting for the ache to return.

But here, now, she let it go. The quilt smelled faintly of the sun.

The house behind her settled with a small creak, like someone shifting their weight in a chair.

She didn't turn. Whatever it was — memory, presence, or something more — it wasn't trying to scare her.

179

It was just... keeping her company.

CHAPTER 15

No problem except where to be happiest

The smell of Old Bay hit her as soon as she got out of the truck. Salt, spice, and firewood drifted on the breeze, pulling her back to every backyard gathering she could remember — kids by the dock checking the crab trap, hands slick with butter, plastic cups sweating in the heat.

A radio played somewhere behind the house — the crackle of an announcer calling the baseball game before someone turned it down and switched to music. She could hear the soft pop of a beer cap, the clatter of tongs against a pot lid, the familiar music of summer starting up again.

Ashley was already on the porch, waving her over with one hand and holding two longnecks in the other. Morgan didn't even have time to knock before the screen door opened and a wave of voices spilled out — laughter, music, someone shouting that it was ready.

"Glad you made it," Ashley said, handing her a beer and brushing a hand across Morgan's back as she passed. The touch was quick, casual. Familiar. The kind that made it feel like no time had passed.

Morgan caught the faint smell of coconut lotion on her skin — or maybe it was just the memory of one — and felt something small loosen in her chest.

Before she could make it out the back door, Morgan heard her name.

"Miss Morgan, is that you?" came a voice from the hallway.

She turned and smiled as Ashley's mom walked in, wiping her hands on a dish towel.

"Lord, it's been too long."

Morgan stepped into the hug without hesitation. "Hi, Mrs. Shirley."

Ashley's dad followed behind, not as tall as she remembered, but with the same gravelly voice.

"Well, I'll be damned."

"Hi, Mr. Harold," she said, and hugged him too. "Y'all haven't changed a bit."

Ashley's mom laughed. "That's a lie, but we'll take it. You hungry?"

"Starving," Morgan said. "And it smells incredible."

Ashley reappeared beside her and nodded toward the back door.

The backyard was lit with strings of white bulbs stretched from tree to tree, casting a warm, lazy glow over the deck and picnic tables. A folding table held two heaping trays of local shrimp as big as Morgan's palm, corn, sausage, and potatoes, steaming under the yellowish light. Paper towels and hot-sauce bottles were wedged between rolls of paper and homemade dishes that always tasted better from this part of the country.

Somebody cranked the burner under the next pot and the air hissed with steam. The whole yard smelled alive — butter, beer, and salt. Fireflies blinked low between the trees like punctuation.

Somewhere near the fence, someone sprayed down the patio with a garden hose, the smell of damp earth rising through the charcoal — a scent that always meant home.

Morgan followed Ashley down the steps, weaving past cousins, neighbors, and two kids chasing each other with water guns. Someone had set up speakers near the fence — Sam Cooke was playing, low and easy, like he was glad to be there too.

They stood side by side, shoulder to shoulder, peeling shrimp and licking the spicy butter from their fingers. Morgan laughed with her mouth full. Ashley told a story about her dad setting the deck umbrella on fire when he was grilling last Fourth of July.

When Morgan laughed, Ashley looked at her longer than the joke required. It wasn't heat exactly, more recognition — the quick spark of seeing someone you've known in every version of yourself.

It was easy in a way that made her chest ache — like remembering something too clearly.

When Ashley's fingers brushed hers while reaching for the same piece of corn, neither of them moved away. But nothing more passed between them. It was just a moment. Like so many they used to have.

By the time they sat down at the edge of the deck, Morgan had that easy kind of fullness — the kind that came from good food and the sound of people talking over each other.

Someone's uncle told a story too loud; a baby cried once then stopped; the cicadas lifted their chorus like an encore. Morgan felt folded into the noise in the best possible way.

Ashley's uncle made a toast with a half-empty beer. Someone started a game of cornhole near the shed. The evening had warmed just enough to make you forget it was still spring. It felt like summer had snuck in a little early, just to see how it fit.

Ashley leaned close. "Pool's probably warm-ish by now."

Morgan glanced toward the far end of the yard, where the pool sat half in shadow. "You serious?"

Ashley grinned. "Well… warm enough for our feet. Come on."

Ashley reached down, grabbed Morgan's hand, and they disappeared around the side of the house without a word to anyone.

Morgan felt the calluses at the base of Ashley's fingers — small, work-hardened — the thought raced in her mind for a brief second that it was ok to come back. She didn't need to earn her way back anymore; the place already knew her.

The sky had settled into that soft cobalt blue that comes just before dark, and the pool lights had flickered on — casting ripples of gold across the water.

Ashley was already sitting on the edge with her feet in the shallow end.

Morgan kicked off her shoes, sat beside her, and dipped her toes in. She hissed through her teeth. "This is not warm."

Ashley smirked. "You get used to it after the first five minutes."

"That's because of the hypothermia."

Ashley laughed and leaned back on her hands. "You always used to drift to the edges at stuff like this," she said. "I remember that from high-school parties. You'd be the first to show up and the last to leave, but somehow still outside it all."

Morgan smiled. "Was it that obvious?"

"Only to me."

Morgan looked down at the water. "Quiet corners."

Ashley nodded. "Yeah. That was you."

They sat with their reflections stretching and breaking in the light ripples, two shapes that almost touched. The frogs had started in the ditch nearby, a low, rhythmic sound that somehow kept time with their breathing.

They sat in silence for a while, legs in the water almost to their knees, the low hum of the party still floating over the yard. The music shifted — Otis Redding now, something slow and full of ache.

Ashley tilted her head back and sighed. "We should probably head back soon if we want any part of that dessert table."

Morgan nodded but didn't move. "Just a minute."

They stayed like that — the air cooling around them, porch lights dancing across the water.

A single moth circled the nearest bulb until it gave up and drifted toward the dark. The sound of laughter carried, then faded. The stillness between them wasn't empty; it hummed.

Later, Morgan sat with Ashley on the porch swing while the party slowly wound down.

Empty trays had been cleared. The kids were inside watching a movie. Someone was packing up folding chairs, stacking them beside the cooler.

Ashley's mom brought out slices of lemon pound cake on paper plates and didn't say a word. She just smiled and squeezed Morgan's shoulder before heading back inside.

They ate in companionable silence, the swing creaking softly beneath them.

Ashley leaned back, her shoulder brushing lightly against Morgan's. "You doing okay?"

Morgan nodded. "Yeah. I think I am."

She meant it. For the first time in a long while, she didn't have to convince herself.

The spring air was thick with charcoal, sweet grass, and something just barely blooming. Somewhere, a frog started its evening song. A screen door banged once and then stayed closed.

Morgan glanced over and saw Ashley watching her again — not like she was waiting for anything, just seeing her. Remembering.

Morgan smiled. Not the kind she used to fake when people asked how she was. The real kind.

Ashley just smiled back, steady as ever. Nothing more needed to be said.

The swing rocked once more, slow and steady, as the night pressed close around them — soft, alive, and full.

CHAPTER 16

The thing that's in you

The yellow pad was already on the table, her pencil resting in the fold. Morgan had made the coffee, sat down, and started writing — not because she felt inspired, but because something inside her had finally stilled. No distractions. No excuses. Just the quiet and the page. The house settled around her like it approved.

She wrote a line. Then another. The story didn't announce itself — it just started to show up, one image at a time. It didn't feel like fiction. But it didn't feel like her, either. It was something in between. Maybe that's what this kind of writing was.

She'd never let herself try before. Not really. She could write an article, sure — knock out a clean 1,200 words on deadline without blinking. She could interview, distill, summarize, turn someone else's mess into something sharp and readable.

But a book? That was something different. Something sacred, and she'd always been afraid to touch it. No matter how many times people said she had talent — professors, family, coworkers, even strangers who'd written in to praise a feature piece — the voice in her head had always been louder. The one that said: You'll never be that good. Not like him. You're not Papa.

Her Granddad's voice would come next, the one that lived in her bones — kind, but clear:

"Never walk in somebody else's shadow. There's no happiness there. You got your own light. Just figure out where to shine it."

She hadn't believed him. Not then.

But maybe today she didn't need to believe anything. Maybe it was enough just to try.

She took a sip of coffee and turned the page. The words came slower now, but she didn't stop. She didn't overthink. She just followed the thread, even when it doubled back on itself or slipped beneath the surface. It didn't matter if it was good. It didn't matter if it made sense. The only thing that mattered was that it was hers.

There had been so many years where she couldn't even open the file — where the thought of starting felt like a setup for failure. Every idea came pre-loaded with self-doubt. Every sentence dragged behind it the weight of everything she'd already decided she wasn't.

But today felt different. Not lighter. Just clearer.

She could almost hear the scratch of her pencil the way she used to hear rain on the roof — steady, unhurried, each sound proof that she was still here.

She realized she didn't owe anyone a story that worked on paper. She didn't need a pitch. A logline. A tidy arc. She just needed to tell the truth the way it lived in her. No deadlines. No editors. No one watching. Just a woman, a pencil, and the quiet of a house that allowed her to be quiet too.

She paused long enough to stretch her back and noticed how the light had changed. It had started out silver and soft. Now it was cutting across the table in sharper lines. The morning was already folding into afternoon. She didn't mind. She didn't want to stop. Not yet.

By the time she looked up again, her coffee had gone cold. Her hand ached. The pad was nearly half full. She hadn't moved in hours.

It wasn't until she stood up that she felt it — that weight in her chest. Not sharp or sudden. Just there.

Writing had always been the dream she didn't name out loud. The one she'd packed away under other people's expectations — and then under her own.

She hadn't expected it to come with this much ache.

It felt like stretching a muscle she hadn't used in years — pain, yes, but also strength waking up.

Morgan crossed to the sink and dumped the rest of her coffee. She rinsed the mug, set it gently in the rack, and just... stood there. One hand on the edge of the counter. Letting the silence move in again.

She'd done the thing she was most afraid of, but it hadn't brought relief. Not yet. It brought memory. Emotion. A kind of hum just beneath the skin. Like something in her had come loose. Or something in the house had started paying closer attention.

She stepped away from the sink and moved through the living room, not really thinking about where she was headed. The windows were open. Just enough to let the air move through. The breeze stirring the edge of the curtain, carried in a trace of salt and damp bark. Out past the trees, the marsh swayed like it always did — calm, indifferent.

Morgan crossed her arms and stood barefoot on the cool floor, her shoulder just barely touching the doorframe. She felt worn out. Like something inside her had been worked over. Not tired. But emptied in a good way. The kind of empty that made room for something else.

Behind her, the floor creaked once — a slow, weighted sound from the hallway.

She didn't turn around. Not because she was scared. But because she didn't want to break the moment. It felt special.

For a heartbeat, she thought she caught the faint scent of tobacco — gone as soon as she noticed it — and smiled to herself. She stayed there awhile. Just listening. Letting the breeze move through the house and over her skin. It felt earned, somehow. The stillness.

Eventually she moved back into the kitchen and reheated leftovers for dinner. No music. No TV. Just the soft sound of her own breath and the distant rustle of a bird's feathers in the tree near the kitchen.

She washed the dishes and set them in the rack to dry. Then crossed the living room and reached for the lamp beside the couch. The light clicked off and in the same breath Morgan heard the muted music from the far wall —

"Skylark... have you anything to say to me?"

Morgan froze. She didn't know the song. But it felt like a question.

She didn't move. Didn't answer. But the air itself seemed to wait, balanced on that single note — the line between presence and memory blurring again.

197

The house felt like it was listening for her response.

CHAPTER 17

One true sentence

The sky had cleared overnight, leaving everything still and rinsed. Morgan didn't do much. She moved through the house opening windows, letting the light in one room at a time.

The yellow pad still sat on the table, open to the last page she'd written. She didn't read it. Just placed her hand on it for a moment, then closed it gently and left it where it was.

She lingered there longer than she meant to, tracing the groove her pencil had left on the top sheet. There was something comforting in the indentations —

knowing that the words were real even when she couldn't bring herself to read them.

By late morning, the stillness had started to feel too tight. Not heavy, just close. She pulled her phone from the kitchen drawer, thumb hovering above the screen. Then she typed:

Morgan

Hey — you around? Want to grab lunch?

She didn't let herself edit it. Just hit send.

It wasn't two minutes before the reply came through:

Ashley

Let's go to The Dockhouse. It's behind the marina — used to be the old boat rental. You'll like it.

Morgan smiled. It was the kind of place that wouldn't have existed when she lived here — too quirky, too casual. But it sounded like something Ashley would love.

She could almost picture Ashley there already — hair tucked behind one ear, laughing with the owner about the day's catch, her sleeves rolled just high enough to show the tan lines of work. That image tugged at something in Morgan that felt half-longing, half-recognition.

Morgan

Sounds perfect. See you there in twenty.

She tossed her phone on the couch, pulled on a pair of worn-in cutoffs and slipped on her flip-flops. She grabbed her keys, tied her hair up, and headed out.

The Dockhouse wasn't much to look at from the road — just a long low building with faded gray clapboard siding and a rusted-out hand-painted sign that hung a little funky over the front steps. But as soon as Morgan stepped onto the wooden deck, she felt good.

The sound of gulls. The smell of fried shrimp and fresh oil. Old ceiling fans turning slow above mismatched tables. A soft vinyl crackle playing through a speaker tucked somewhere near the counter.

There were people laughing, barefoot kids trailing sand, someone with a guitar case leaning against the rail. It wasn't trying to be charming. It just was.

She spotted Ashley before Ashley saw her — already sitting at a table near the edge of the dock, sunlight in her hair, a glass of sweet tea sweating in her hand. The water shimmered just beyond the railing, calm and gold-streaked.

Morgan hesitated, then made her way over.

Ashley looked up. Smiled. Not wide. Just enough.

"Hey, you," she said.

Morgan slid into the seat across from her.

"Hey."

Ashley leaned back in her chair, resting the glass against her knee. "Hope you're hungry. I already ordered some stuff. Pimento cheese and fried green tomatoes."

Morgan picked up a napkin and smoothed it across her lap. "Nice. I'm starving."

A server came by and slid the plates onto the table. Everything smelled like a memory. Salt, oil, a hint of garlic.

Morgan nodded and reached for a piece of toast slathered with pimento cheese. She took a slow bite. Sharp, creamy, a little too much — but she didn't mind.

Ashley took a sip from her tea, then said, "They've got an old Wurlitzer inside. Still works." She stood up. "I'll put something on."

Morgan watched her head inside — easy, familiar, like she belonged in a place like this.

A minute later, the music started. Not too loud. Bluesy and dark.

Morgan didn't know the song, but the voice was rough in a good way.

"Take me down, down, down where the black water flows. Drop me down far deep into the sea."

Ashley returned to the table, dropped back into her seat, and picked up a shrimp like nothing had happened.

"You always chose good tunes," Morgan said.

Ashley didn't look up right away. Just nodded, like she'd been waiting to hear that for a long time.

The song kept playing behind them — rough guitar, worn edges, a voice that knew something about leaving and staying anyway. Neither of them spoke for a while. They didn't need to.

When the plates were mostly empty and the sun had shifted just enough to make them squint, Ashley stood and stretched her arms overhead.

"Want to walk a bit?" she asked. "The dock wraps around back — usually quieter there."

"Sure," Morgan replied, pushing back her chair.

They walked side by side without saying much. The boards creaked under their feet. A pelican drifted low over the water and disappeared beyond the reeds.

Morgan caught herself matching Ashley's stride, hearing the boards creak in rhythm with their steps. The air smelled like diesel from the shrimp boats mixed with the sweetness of sun-baked wood — a scent that belonged entirely to the Low Country. She thought about all the stories she'd never written about this place because she didn't trust herself to match in words what this felt like.

Down at the end of the dock, someone had set out two rocking chairs — salt-worn.

Ashley leaned on the railing, looking out toward the far bank.

"I used to come out here by myself. Before it got busy."

Morgan eased down into one of the rocking chairs, stretching her legs out in front of her. The wood was warm from the sun, smooth in that way old things get from time and salt air.

Ashley stayed at the rail, her fingers curled loosely over the edge.

"You ever think about staying gone?" Morgan asked. "Like... for good?"

Ashley's head tilted just slightly, like she was weighing the question. "I did stay gone. For a while."

"I mean the kind where you don't even look back."

Ashley didn't answer right away. She was quiet long enough that Morgan almost let the question drift off.

Then: "There's always something that pulls you back. Even if it's just a memory. Or a place. Or..." She stopped there.

Morgan rocked once, slow and steady.

"Or a person."

Ashley looked over her shoulder. Met Morgan's eyes.

It hit Morgan how much she'd missed being looked at like that — not judged, not evaluated, just seen. The kind of look that asked nothing and offered everything in return. It made her wonder if all this time she hadn't been running from loneliness so much as from the possibility of being known.

"Yeah," Ashley said quietly. "That too."

The breeze picked up, just enough to stir Ashley's shirt against her ribs, just enough to make Morgan feel the edge of something unsaid pulling tight between them.

Ashley turned back toward the water.

"I used to think leaving was the brave thing."

"And now?"

"Now I think maybe staying is. If you can manage to stay and keep your soul."

Morgan didn't respond, just leaned her head back and looked up at the pale sky. A gull cut across the open blue, silent as it passed.

Ashley finally moved to the chair beside her, not quite sitting — just resting her hand on the back of it, fingers tapping lightly along the slat.

"I should get back soon," she said. "Inventory and invoices."

Morgan smiled without opening her eyes.

"That glamorous hardware life."

"Exactly."

A pause. Then, a little softer:

"I'm glad you texted."

Morgan sat up again. "Me too."

Ashley didn't move yet. Just stayed there, hand on the chair, like maybe she wanted to say something else but couldn't quite find the words.

Then she gave Morgan's shoulder the lightest squeeze — more steadying than affectionate — and said,

"See you soon, alright?"

"Yeah," Morgan said. "Soon."

Ashley walked back down the dock, sunlight catching in her hair, shoulders set just a little looser now.

Morgan watched her go. The quiet settled in again — a little lonelier than before.

A small skiff cut across the creek, its wake rippling toward the dock. Morgan waited for the water to settle befcre she stood. She glanced at the empty chair beside her and thought how every conversation between them still felt like a beginning. Then she slipped her hands into her pockets and walked back toward the truck, the sound of gulls rising behind her like applause.

CHAPTER 18

The rain stopped and the world was quiet

Morgan didn't go straight home.

She took the long way instead, windows down, one arm resting along the open frame. The air still held warmth from earlier, but the wind was cooling — a late afternoon kind of change, all hush and hint.

She passed the marina again, then the road that curled toward the overlook. Farther on, the old bait stand sat boarded up beside a crooked sign that once read LIVE BAIT in red paint. Someone had scratched out the "live" years ago. Now it just said BAIT.

The radio had been silent for most of the drive. But just before the turn onto the back road home, she found a signal — a low hum, a bit of static — and then, soft and steady, a voice came through.

"Down here, the river meets the sea..."

John Hiatt. Rough around the edges, warm in the middle. Like somebody singing from the bottom of a whiskey glass.

Morgan didn't touch the dial.

"Feels like rain..."

She eased off the gas.

The road curved through a stretch of trees, and the light slipped sideways through the branches. Every turn brought something she remembered — the fence where Ashley carved her initials, the ditch they'd jump when the field flooded, the fire tower they dared each other to climb. Neither ever made it all the way.

And the younger version of herself too — the one who rode her bicycle from the candy store to the hardware store and down every dirt road she and Ashley could find.

The song kept going, slow and sure.

"And it feels like rain..."

She didn't feel sadness exactly. Just the kind of ache that comes from remembering what used to be — and actually letting yourself feel it.

For the first time, she didn't flinch from it. Memory wasn't something to escape anymore; it was something to sit beside, like an old friend who still knew your laugh.

By the time she turned onto the dirt road home, the day had gone quiet again. The hum of the tires over gravel filled the space the radio didn't. Every so often, a bird lifted from the brush and disappeared into the trees. The stillness didn't bother her — it just felt full, like the air was holding its breath.

She turned off the engine and sat for a moment, both hands still on the wheel. Not to think. Not to plan. Just to feel.

Then she stepped out, walked up the steps, and let the screen door swing shut behind her.

The Bar was silent.

Inside, the air had cooled while she was gone. Not cold, just a few degrees lower than she left it — like the house had exhaled while she was away.

She moved through the front room without turning on a light. Let the dim hang around her shoulders a while.

The yellow pad was still on the table. Pencil tucked into the spiral. She didn't look at it long. Just passed by and let her fingers trail across the edge.

In the kitchen, she poured a glass of water and stood at the sink while she drank. The faucet dripped once behind her, a single tick in the stillness. She didn't move to fix it.

Down the hall, she could see the closet door had worked itself open again — not wide, just a sliver. Enough to notice. Enough to remind.

She didn't check it right away. Just stood there, letting her eyes adjust.

A corner of something soft had spilled out — a blanket, maybe. Or an old coat sleeve. She walked over slowly, crouched, and pushed the edge back in. But when her hand brushed the floor, it hit something solid.

Morgan paused. Pulled the blanket aside.

A shoebox. Taped shut, edges worn and flaking at the corners. No label. No writing. Just a brittle strip of masking tape across the top.

She lifted it. Light. But not empty.

She set it on the dining table. Didn't open it.

Not yet.

The air in the room changed — not colder or darker, just charged, like a current waiting for ground. The walls seemed to hold still, listening.

She poured a second glass of water. Turned off the kitchen light.

Then sat down across from it in the dark.

She peeled the tape back — slow and careful — and lifted the lid.

The box wasn't packed full. A tiny pocket New Testament. A leather change pouch. An empty, crushed box of cherry Ludens — the kind Granddad used to eat like candy in church. And a small pocket notebook, opened to a page that read, in pencil:

$80 no less.

No telling what that was about, but apparently Granddad had something to sell and he wasn't going to take a dime under eighty.

She moved the items aside, one at a time, not sure what she was looking for.

Near the bottom, tucked flat against the cardboard, was a folded square of soft white cotton.

She picked it up carefully.

A handkerchief. One of his. Monogrammed in the corner — WBL — the stitching nearly worn through from age and use.

He always carried these. She remembered the way he'd press one into her hands when she was little and crying — sometimes dabbing at her face himself if she couldn't manage. Runny noses. Skinned knees. Hurt feelings.

She held it to her face.

Lavender.

Not the perfume kind. The real stuff. Dried from the plant outside the kitchen door and tucked in a jar of rice to keep the smell.

She lifted it to her nose out of habit. The scent was still there, faint but stubborn. It hit her harder than she expected.

Lavender was comfort. How had she forgotten that?

Her throat tightened, but she didn't cry. She just held the cloth a little tighter, smoothing the wrinkles like she was straightening something in herself.

She stood, crossed to the cabinet above the fridge, and pulled down the bottle. Poured two fingers into a glass. No ice.

She took a slow sip, the bourbon tracing warmth through her chest. Outside, the first crickets started up — faint, uneven.

She came back to the table.

Set the glass beside the handkerchief.

Then sat without speaking.

The Bar held her steady, the quiet stretching between her and whatever remained — memory, spirit, or something beyond both. Outside, a night bird called once and went still, like punctuation on a story she wasn't ready to finish.

CHAPTER 19

You belong to me and all Paris

She didn't sleep much.

Not because she was upset. Not exactly. Just... turned over. Restless in a way that felt physical.

Outside, the sky hadn't opened yet, but the air already smelled like rain.

She'd kept the handkerchief on the table, next to the bourbon glass — both of them still there when she passed through the kitchen just after seven. She didn't touch either. Just glanced at them once before making her morning trek out onto the porch.

The sky was a muted gray, all flat light and slow cloud movement. Not stormy yet — but not far off. The kind of morning that carried weight without urgency.

She sat on the top step watching a lizard make its slow way along the porch rail. Every so often it stopped, puffed its throat, and moved again.

Her phone buzzed from inside.

She didn't move at first. Let it buzz again. Then again.

When she finally went to check it, there was a string of three messages from Margaret.

Margaret

You alive out there?

Storm's gonna hit overnight.

If you need to come into town, do it early.

Morgan smiled without meaning to.

Morgan

Doing ok, Aunt Margaret. I'm all set. Let me know if you need anything.

She didn't hit send right away.

Instead, she looked out the window, toward the bend in the marsh where the tide was beginning to pull back. Everything felt slower today. Heavier, but not bad.

She hit send. Then set the phone facedown on the counter and let the silence stretch again.

The clouds thickened as the morning went on, softening the light until everything looked a little flatter. A little closer.

Not dark — just dim, like a nightlight.

Morgan opened a few of the windows wider, let the breeze move through the house. It smelled like river water and pine and something cooler underneath — a change coming.

She walked through the kitchen slowly. The coffee had gone cold, but she didn't bother refreshing it. She wasn't really drinking it anyway.

In the living room, one of the older windows rattled faintly in its frame. Not from wind, exactly — just the way the house adjusted to the day.

She pulled her hair up, twisted it into a knot, and grabbed a hoodie off the hook by the door. Then stepped out into the yard barefoot, toes curling in the damp grass.

The trees were restless — not wild, just muttering. Cypress needles whispering overhead. The sky had dulled to a pale pewter, and she could smell the rain, even though it hadn't started yet.

She circled around the back of the house, where the ground stayed soft even in dry weather. A couple of shingles had come loose on the shed roof — she made a mental note to try to have the roof checked before the real weather came.

Everything felt like it was holding its breath.

She didn't mind it.

Back inside, the house felt cooler. The breeze through the windows had picked up just enough to stir the edge of the curtain in the hallway. A soft flutter, back and forth. Nothing dramatic. But it made her pause.

She stood there for a moment, hand resting lightly on the doorframe, listening. Not for anything in particular. Just... mindful.

The house made its usual sounds — the old boards stretching, the slow creak of the walls. But today, it all felt closer. Like the house was breathing just beneath the surface.

She walked to the table and moved the handkerchief, folding it carefully and tucking it into the drawer beside the bed. Not to hide it — just to keep it safe.

The bourbon glass was still there, nearly empty. She rinsed it and set it in the rack.

It wasn't until she turned to leave the kitchen that she noticed the music.

Faint. Almost not there.

She held still.

But the sound was there — low, distant. A few piano notes. Something old.

She crossed into the living room slowly. It kept playing just for a moment.

Then it stopped.

Morgan waited, still and quiet, heart not racing but aware.

She stood there for a long time before saying anything. And even then, it was barely a whisper.

"Okay."

She wasn't sure if she was answering herself or the house.

She didn't move. Just stood there, facing the turntable, hands loose at her sides.

Nothing about the room had changed. The lamp on the side table still cast its warm pool of light. The floorboard under the window still creaked when the wind hit the house just right. Everything looked exactly the same.

But it didn't feel the same.

She walked over slowly and lowered the lid of the turntable. Pressed her palm flat against the top — just enough to feel the cool of it.

Nothing buzzed beneath her hand.

She stepped back. Crossed her arms over her chest. Waited a few more seconds, like the house might offer up an explanation.

It didn't.

Morgan turned away and walked to the kitchen. She picked up a glass from the rack

filled it with water and drank it standing at the sink.

When she glanced toward the hall again, the curtain was still moving.

She didn't go check the window. She already knew it was closed.

She didn't bother with the closet either. Not today.

Instead, she grabbed the old metal flashlight from the hall cabinet — the one with the chipped red handle and the piece of duct tape holding the battery compartment shut — and turned it over in her hands.

Still worked.

She set it on the counter, then moved through the house slowly, checking latches, nudging windows almost-closed. Not tight, just enough to keep the air from turning on her while she slept.

Outside, the wind picked up. Pine needles scratched softly against the roof. The sound of rain just out of reach.

She clicked on a lamp in the living room and left the overhead lights off.

On the coffee table, she set down her water glass — not really thinking. Just letting the house settle again. Letting herself match its pace.

She left the pad open. Turned off the lamp.

But didn't go to bed.

She sat back down on the couch, pulled the blanket higher over her legs, and let the house go quiet around her.

Her phone buzzed once beside her.

Ashley

Hey. Remember when I cut my foot on glass at the beach? You gave me a piggyback ride all the way home. You swore I was being dramatic.

Morgan smiled before she even finished reading.

Morgan

You WERE being dramatic. You were hardly bleeding. Honestly, I think it was a shell and you were just tired of walking.

Ashley replied right away:

Ashley

I wasn't tired! I was wounded and you knew it or you wouldn't have carried me.

Nobody babies me anymore. It's just me being pitiful alone.

A few seconds later:

Ashley

I'm so glad you're home.

There is literally nobody else in the world I can do this with.

I've missed it.

Morgan didn't answer right away.

She just rested the phone against her chest, eyes on the ceiling, letting the weight of it land.

Then typed:

Me too.

They kept texting after that, for hours like teenagers. Catching up as well as you can after years missed.

The storm rolled in quietly above them. The house settled deeper into itself. The world stayed dim and close.

By the time Morgan set the phone facedown beside her, the wind had eased again. The rain hadn't started yet, but it was close. Everything in the air felt hushed.

She leaned back into the couch, one arm tucked beneath the blanket, the other resting across her chest.

She didn't text.

Didn't write.

Just sat there and let the thought take shape.

Outside, the first drops of rain hit the porch roof, soft as fingertips.

I love you. Maybe she'd say it out loud one day.

CHAPTER 20

See you in my dreams

The music was already playing when Morgan opened her eyes in the dark.

Faint, but unmistakable. She looked at the clock: 2:43 a.m.

The house was quiet now, still at the edge of sleep, but she could almost hear the tail end of the song fading into nothing.

"This is your hometown.

Yourrrr homeeee townnnn".

She sat up slowly and rubbed her eyes. She knew the music had been real — not a dream — just a voice, familiar rising from the haze of sleep. Rough-edged. Hurting.

She didn't turn on a light. Didn't check the console. She just let the house be still.

She went back to the bedroom — her bedroom now — and pulled the quilt up around her shoulders. The room no longer felt like his. Not entirely. She glanced once toward the door, half-expecting to hear something more, but the silence held. Still, the air felt different, like someone had been there a moment ago.

She closed her eyes. The voice — wherever it had come from — was gone now, but it had left something behind. Not fear. Just the familiar weight of not feeling entirely alone. She didn't know what to do with that, so she let it be.

Morgan didn't move right away. She lay still beneath the quilt, eyes closed, one arm tucked behind her head. The bedroom was warm enough, touched by the first stretch of light through the curtains, but she didn't feel pulled toward the day just yet.

She thought about the music. Not the melody — that had already faded — but the feeling of it. The tone of the voice. The ache in it. It hadn't scared her; it had stirred something. Something old, maybe.

She hadn't been dreaming. She was sure of that. She'd opened her eyes to the sound, and for a few seconds it had felt like someone was sitting beside the bed, just listening with her. But when she'd sat up, there was nothing. No record spinning. No trace of sound. Only the stillness of the room and the quiet weight of whatever had passed through it.

She took a deep breath, then let it go. She pushed back the quilt and sat on the edge of the bed, bare feet brushing the floor. The quiet held — soft and unbothered. She stood, stretched, and moved toward the kitchen, pausing in the hallway to touch the doorframe with her fingertips as she passed, not for any reason, just out of habit.

The kettle took a little longer than usual to boil. Or maybe she was simply more awake for it this time. She didn't put on a record or open a window; she just stood there, watching the water begin to move.

When it finally whistled, she poured it over the coffee grounds and leaned against the counter, holding the mug in both hands. No plans yet. No list. Just the warmth — and the steady way the light kept finding its way across the floor. The water pressure in the shower was still strong, even with the older pipes. She let it beat down over her shoulders, eyes closed, hands resting against the tile. No music. No thinking. Just the simple rhythm of it.

She toweled off, pulled on a soft T-shirt and a pair of cutoff sweatpants, and walked barefoot back through the hallway. Her phone was ringing by the time she reached the kitchen. She caught it just before it went to voicemail.

"Aunt Margaret?"

There was a pause on the line. "Morning, honey. You up?"

"Barely. What's going on?"

"It's Mr. Truluck," Margaret said gently. "He passed away last night. In his sleep."

Morgan leaned against the counter, phone warm against her ear. "Aw, no. Really? I just talked to him."

"I know. He was doing okay, far as anybody could tell. I guess it was just time."

Morgan was quiet for a second. "When's the funeral?"

"Monday morning, I think. At First Baptist. I'll double-check and let you know. Thought maybe we could go together, if you wanted."

"Yeah," Morgan said softly. "Let's do that. Thanks for letting me know."

They said goodbye. Morgan poured the rest of her coffee down the sink and stood there a moment longer. The house didn't feel different exactly, but it held a new kind of stillness now.She sent a quick text to Ashley:

Morgan

Hey — just heard Mr. Truluck passed.

A minute went by. Then another.

Ashley

Yeah. Just heard too. It's sad. He was a sweet man.

I'm at the store all day. If you're out, come by.

Morgan set the phone down and looked toward the window. The sky was a soft slate color, the kind that pressed low over the marsh but never felt heavy. She thought about how, just a few days ago, Mr. Truluck had been sitting in that same old chair outside the store, eyes half-closed against the sun, remembering her birthday.

It didn't make sense how quickly people could vanish from a place and still leave it full of their shape.

She rinsed her mug, took her keys, and stood for a moment by the door. The air outside smelled faintly of salt and something sweet — like honeysuckle clinging to the edge of the season.

She took the long way — the one that hugged the marsh and cut through the thin corridor of trees. The road shimmered slightly in places where the rain had teased but never landed. Spanish moss hung low, brushing the roof of her truck like slow-moving fog.

She drove with one hand on the wheel, the other resting on the open window frame. The radio stayed off. The only sound was the hum of the tires and the far-off rhythm of the tide.

Every few miles she passed something that felt like memory: the old shrimp shack with its paint sun-bleached to near-white, the leaning mailbox with the name Drummond still half-visible in faded blue. Each one its own kind of ghost story, only quieter.

She didn't feel lonely. Just aware — of these familiar, old places and the people who once cared for them.

By the time she crossed the bridge into town, the sun was slipping through a break in the clouds, laying down streaks of gold across the river. She slowed at the light, hand tapping the steering wheel in time with a song that wasn't playing.

When she turned into the grocery lot, the world felt smaller again — not in a bad way, just contained. She parked beneath the overhang, the smell of hot, wet asphalt rising as she stepped out. Truluck's would be closed today, of course, so she went to the larger grocery down by the bridge. She picked up a few things for the week and, on impulse, grabbed a Red Rock Strawberry Soda in a glass bottle.

There was a display near the front with fresh-baked goods from a local bakery. She picked the best-looking donut from the batch — thick with glaze and still slightly warm — and had it boxed up.

Morgan pulled into the lot beside Harbor Iron & Tool, the soda and donut still sitting on the passenger seat. Ashley's SUV was parked out front.

Morgan stepped inside. The bell above the door gave its usual half-hearted, happy jingle.

Ashley looked up from behind the counter, her hair pulled back, sleeves rolled, a pencil still tucked behind that ear. She smiled when she saw Morgan — a little tired, still warm.

"Hey," she said.

Morgan crossed the floor and set the bottle and small white bag on the counter. "Didn't figure you'd had brunch yet."

Ashley laughed. "Nope — had to miss brunch these past five years or so."

She blinked at the soda. "Red Rock? Where'd you even find that?"

"Town grocery. Hiding behind the Cheerwine."

Ashley grinned, and for a second she looked like the girl Morgan remembered — same easy laugh, same wide eyes.

"This is perfect," she said, pulling the bottle closer. "And exactly what I needed."

Morgan shrugged. "Didn't have time to whip up an Eggs Benedict this morning."

Ashley reached for the donut bag. "Ohhh, this is even better. Thank you."

Morgan offered a small wave. "I'll get out of your hair. Just wanted to drop it off."

Ashley gave her a look that landed gently. "I'm really glad you did."

Morgan nodded once and turned back toward the door.

The bell jingled as she stepped out into the light.

CHAPTER 21

Let me whisper in your ear

A few days later, Morgan stood at the kitchen counter, drying her hands on a dish towel. The dishes were done. Outside, the light had gone late-afternoon gold. The cabin was quiet. It was the good kind of quiet — not hollow, just still.

She walked to the console and pulled out Déjà Vu. She hadn't played it in years, but something about the day felt like it could hold it — the harmonies, the ache. She cued up the record and lowered the needle. A brief crackle gave way to guitar and voices, layered and low, curling into the corners of the room like smoke.

She opened the front window a few inches. The air that drifted in was now full of jasmine and the faint tang of salt. A breeze lifted the edge of the curtain and let it fall again.

The drawer beneath the kitchen phone had become her next small project. Junk drawers were like time capsules — never meant to be opened, exactly, but full of things nobody wanted to throw away. She pulled everything out and spread it across the table: rubber bands melted together, a dozen twist ties, dead batteries, stamps with curled corners.

And then — a keychain. Faded red leather with a tarnished brass bottle opener on the back. She flipped it over and read the embossed logo:

Knowles Armory & Range — Summerville, SC.

She turned it in her hand, thumb tracing the worn edge.

"Yes," she said aloud. "Won't have to use that old dinosaur from the drawer anymore."

She hung it from the nail by the porch door, just below the light switch — the kind of thing you don't think about, but always ends up close by.

Behind her, the song shifted — Crosby's voice rising through Helpless. The harmonies caught somewhere in her chest and stayed. She glanced toward the hallway — not afraid, not expectant. Just aware.

The house felt like it was listening.

Later, she changed clothes, pulled her hair back, and decided to organize the linen closet. Inside: towels, mismatched sheets, a heating pad with a tangled cord, a stack of faded pillowcases. Nothing strange — just stale. She left the door cracked to let it breathe.

By dusk, the light had cooled. Long shadows reached across the porch floor. She poured another cup of coffee and stepped outside, letting the screen door snap shut behind her. The brass keychain caught the last bit of sun. She tapped it once with her fingertip and sat down.

Out across the marsh, the horizon had gone to blue — the kind of blue that meant the day was done. After dinner, she curled up on the couch and turned on the

TV — something she did less often these days. She landed on a special about Doo-Wop groups and early '60s rock.

The voice-over was warm, familiar. Archival footage rolled by — drive-in diners, ferry crossings, city buses full of kids in Sunday clothes. A band played low and slow beneath it — maybe a Drifters B-side, maybe something rarer.

She lay back and watched until the colors blurred.

The program shifted to an interview with a retired radio DJ from Charleston. His voice was gravelly and kind — the sort of voice made for nighttime. He talked about late-night dedications and the sound of a needle drop.

Morgan pulled the quilt across her lap and let herself drift. Not asleep. Just untethered.

The TV glowed in the corner. The DJ faded out. A new montage rolled — neon signs, long two-lane roads at dusk. Southern nights. The kind that felt humid even through the screen.

She stayed there, letting it wash over her.

A black-and-white clip of a jukebox clicked through selections, then cut to a segment on regional radio in the 1960s. Soft music played underneath — familiar, but out of reach.

She leaned back and let her eyes close.

Then — beneath the TV's low hum — a melody came forward.

Just a few bars of something she almost knew.

"Listen...

Do you want to know a secret?

Do you promise not to tell...

Whoa-oh-oh..."

And then it warped.

Not just the pitch — the pace itself. Like a record left too long in a hot car. The voice stretched and sagged, each word dragging behind the beat.

"Cloooser..."

From down the hall came a soft click — the sound of a latch giving way.

The hallway closet door.

She sat forward, eyes drawn to the darkened hall.

The music kept playing — slower now, the words slurred and underwater.

"Let me whisperrr in your earrrrr..."

The voice was full of static and something else. Not frightening. But personal. Too close.

She stood. Slowly.

The closet door was shut. Latched.

Hadn't she heard it? That sound — the click and swing of the one door nobody liked to open.

She didn't go to it — not yet.

Just stood there with the quilt around her shoulders, listening.

And then — like someone letting go — the song cut out mid-note.

The screen blinked. A new segment rolled in about church choirs. Bright and clean and unrelated.

Morgan clicked the volume down. She didn't turn the TV off. The air in the room felt different.

She went into the kitchen, took a sip of cold coffee, and set the mug in the sink. Her pulse was steady. But something in her chest felt... opened.

She didn't look down the hall again.

Not tonight.

She stepped onto the porch and let the night meet her face.

The keychain tapped once against the wall.

Then again.

She stilled it with her fingertip and left her hand there, feeling the small vibration of metal against wood.

Beyond the porch, the marsh shimmered with moonlight. Crickets sawed their steady rhythm in the grass, and somewhere far off a boat engine coughed and went quiet. The world had folded into itself, waiting.

Her granddad used to say a house only creaked when it was settling — when the summer air cooled for the night and everything settled back into place. Maybe that was true for people, too. Maybe this was what it meant to settle.

She leaned back in the chair, eyes half-closed, listening as the wind shifted through the palmettos. Her night didn't feel empty anymore.

Morgan smiled into the dark.

"Goodnight, Papa," she whispered.

CHAPTER 22

Two birds, baby!

The next morning, Morgan moved slowly through her routine. The odd happenings of the evening before were still on her mind, but the sun was coming through the kitchen window now — pale and uncomplicated. She swept the porch. Changed the sheets. Tossed a few of the moth-eaten linens into a bag for disposal and folded the good ones a bit neater.

By mid-morning, she'd made a small list: peanut butter, paper towels, a new mop. Nothing pressing, but enough to get her out of the cabin. And there was something else tugging at her — a memory, maybe, or just the idea of a new thread being pulled. She scribbled a few more items on the list and slid it into her back pocket.

The store was quiet when she pulled in. It was the first time she'd stopped in since Mr. Truluck had passed away. Just two other cars out front and the familiar whirr of the old ceiling fan, off balance and audible even through the screen door.

Morgan stepped inside and nodded at the teenager behind the counter — a wiry boy with a ballcap too big for his head. The front room still smelled like a mixture of live crickets from the box right beside the door, boiling peanuts, and bins of sweet penny candy.

She made her way toward the cleaning aisle but stopped when she heard a soft voice call her name.

"Morgan?"

She turned. A woman stood by the coolers near the back, holding a small crate. Her features were sharp, sun-weathered, with gray at her temples and eyes the exact color of Mr. Trulucks. The voice was familiar before the face came into focus — something buried deep in the rhythm of her childhood summers. It took Morgan a second, then it clicked.

"Abigail?" she asked.

The woman smiled. "Didn't think you'd remember."

"Of course I do!" Abigail was the Truluck's oldest daughter who didn't come back as often. She had moved to St. Louis when she married out of college and her life was there now.

They walked toward each other — not quite a hug, but something familiar and warm in the way they greeted.

"I was hoping you'd come by," Abigail said. "Daddy mentioned he saw you one afternoon. He seemed so happy you were back and the Bar was being lived in again."

Morgan smiled, a little sheepish. "He caught me off guard. Still sharp as ever."

Abigail nodded. "He had his days."

Morgan could tell the memory — and the loss — was still floating just beneath the surface.

"Listen, I've got something for you."

She walked to the back office and came out with a small cardboard box.

"I've been going through some old things from Daddy's office — papers, photos. I found this and thought you'd like to have them."

Inside were two old photo envelopes and a slim DVD case.

"I had DVDs made from an old videotape," Abigail said. "Didn't want it to rot away. I think it's footage from The Bar. Maybe a birthday party or get together. Early '90s, I'd guess."

Morgan felt her throat tighten. "Thank you."

Abigail waved it off. "I was making a copy anyway and thought your family would like to have one."

They chatted a little longer — about the town, about how fast things changed, and how some things were immune to it altogether.

Morgan picked up her few items and left the store with the small box cradled in one arm, knowing she was carrying much more than home movies and old photos.

She set the box on the passenger seat and started the truck, but she didn't pull out right away. She just sat there for a minute, both hands on the wheel, thinking about the last time she spoke to Mr. Truluck — the weight of the moment catching up to her. This wasn't just a DVD. It was what it might hold. Faces. Voices. Maybe even Granddad's laugh — that big, round sound she hadn't heard in over twenty years.

Back at The Bar, Morgan put away the groceries and carried the box into the living room.

She pulled her phone from the counter and scrolled to Jimmy's name.

"Hey," she said when he picked up. "You busy?"

"Yes... There's an Andy Griffith marathon on."

"Come on, dude..." Morgan laughed. "Wanna come over? I found something. Actually, Abigail Truluck found something. It's a DVD. From back when. I also need you to bring a DVD player."

There was a pause.

"I'll be there in twenty."

Jimmy pulled in just as the light started to slip sideways — that golden hour that turned everything into a sepia-toned dream. He stepped onto the porch with a six-pack in hand and a big Jimmy grin.

"I brought goodies," he said, holding up the beer, the dusty DVD player tucked under one arm.

"Couldn't run a Swiffer over that thing before leaving the house?" Morgan asked, smirking.

Jimmy shrugged. "What? My shirt dusted it as I was walking. Two birds, baby!"

They settled into the living room — Jimmy on the couch, Morgan cross-legged on the floor like they were twelve again. DVD player connected and disc slid inside.

The screen lit up with the kitchen — the old table, the backs of children's heads, the faint shape of someone else off to the right.

"Wow!" Jimmy said. "I don't remember this.. So weird!"

Morgan recognized most of the kids around the table. She saw herself standing between Jimmy and Jen. The Bar was abuzz with conversation, excited children, and music... always music.

Granddad had apparently let the birthday boy pick the tunes that day.

"Ice, Ice Baby?" Morgan looked over at her wide-grinned cousin.

"What?" he asked. "That song was awesome... in 1991."

Morgan smiled, opened her eyes wide, and shook her head.

They continued to watch their gifted, precious time capsule as the camera was passed around the room — outside as the kids played Red Rover until someone started crying, and then back through the porch and into the living room.

The view panned over to Granddad for a moment, and she felt like her heart was more full right then than she could stand. The lens moved away, but his voice lingered — caught in a background conversation.

"I can't let you borrow that old thing. It's got a terrible hair trigger. I'm taking it down to that place in Summerville. They quoted me eighty bucks so I might as well get it done."

Morgan leaned forward, frowning slightly.

"Wait—" she said, eyes narrowing. "Did you hear what he said?"

She paused the DVD and walked over to the shelf where she had placed the items from the old shoebox. She reached for the notebook and handed it to her cousin, already opened to the page.

Jimmy stared at the words:

$80 — noless

He sat back slowly. "What is this?"

"It's a notepad Granddad had with his stuff. The coroner gave it back to Aunt Margaret and she stuck it in that hall closet. I figured he was selling something — 'no less' made it sound like a price he wouldn't budge on."

The two sat together for a while, continued watching the DVD, and tried to make sense of Granddad's quickly jotted reminder.

Morgan said, "I need a beer and some fresh air. Come on."

They both grabbed a brown bottle from the fridge and walked out to the porch. She took the leather keychain from the nail on the wall and popped the top of her bottle with a hiss. Morgan passed the keychain over, and Jimmy looked at it briefly before opening his beer.

"Where in the world did you find this old thing?"

"Someone left it in the junk drawer in the kitchen."

Morgan looked at the worn leather again.

"Wait a minute, Jim… look at this."

Jimmy took the keychain back and read it aloud. "Knowles Armory and Range — Summerville, SC."

He looked back to Morgan, smiling.

"This is the place he was going. It has to be. Let me see the notebook again."

Morgan reached into her pocket and passed the small book over.

For a second, the air between them stilled — the kind of quiet that comes right before something clicks into place.

"Mor…look at this. $80 noless. How much you want to bet he called this place to get an estimate on the repair, grabbed this out of his pocket, and wrote it down when he found a pencil? You know how he was… this isn't $80 no less — it's $80 Knowles. It's a quote for a repair."

Morgan stared at the words, the meaning falling into place so fast it almost made her dizzy. Then, like exhaling after years of holding her breath, she laughed.

They both laughed at the confusion that was so completely Granddad.

After a while, Morgan got up and put the DVD back in its case.

"There's more to watch. Wanna finish it later — when Margaret and the rest are here?"

Jimmy nodded. "I think that's a great idea. Everyone should get to enjoy it. You want some dinner?"

"I was thinking pizza," she said.

"Perfect."

They ended up eating on the porch, paper plates balanced on their knees. Jimmy talked about work, about his sister Jenn's new dog, about how Truluck's now carried kombucha for some reason.

"Nobody in this town is gonna know what that is except Abigail Truluck," he said. "She'll spend more time explaining what's in it than actually selling any of it."

Morgan laughed. It felt easy. Like she could breathe deeper out here — like something had finally let go.

When the porch light flicked on automatically, Jimmy glanced toward the door.

"You ever think this place is trying to tell you something?"

"Sometimes," Morgan said. "But that particular hint was just the motion lights I put in last week."

Jimmy smiled. "Smart ass."

Morgan smiled and looked out toward the dark marsh, the night soft and forgiving around them.

CHAPTER 23

The light of the afternoon was on her face

The humidity had settled in overnight — thick and unmoving. When Morgan woke, a fine sweat clung to her collarbone, and the sheets felt heavy, damp at the edges.

The air in the bedroom was still. Not unbearable, but enough to make her sit up and turn on the fan. She swung her legs over the side of the bed and sat for a minute, listening.

No sounds but the soft tick of the kitchen clock down the hall and a distant hum outside — maybe insects, maybe the neighbor's dock pump — she couldn't tell. She rubbed a hand across her face, then stood and pulled her hair into a rough knot, already sensing the day would be a sticky one.

In the kitchen, she poured water into the kettle and opened the screen door to see what she had to look forward to. The porch boards creaked like they always did, and the smell of the marsh drifted in with the rising heat — sweet, green, and just a little sour.

She stepped out barefoot, cup in hand, and leaned against the railing. The air was thick, and she already felt like she was breathing through wet cotton. Her shirt was clinging to her back, but she didn't mind. Not today.

The memory of last night was still warm in her chest: the sound of Granddad's voice — grainy and real. Jimmy's laugh. That ridiculous note.

Eighty bucks, Knowles. She smiled to herself and sipped her coffee.

It felt good to be alone with it all. Not in a lonely way, but in the way that let her feel tethered — to the past, to something steady that had finally made her feel the ground wasn't shifting beneath her.

Outside, a heron lifted from the edge of the creek, its shadow sliding across the porch boards — one quiet, effortless motion that somehow felt like agreement.

She stepped back inside and shut the screen door behind her with a soft clap. The stillness in the kitchen had turned soupy, the air thick enough to taste.

She stood in front of the thermostat for a second.

"All right," she said out loud, flipping the switch. "I give up."

The old unit kicked on with a low rumble — not the newest model, but Granddad and the groundskeeper had kept it in good shape. Cool air began pushing through the vents with a hiss that sounded like relief itself.

In the living room, she pulled the cord on the ceiling fan and felt the slow churn of air stir above her. It was the kind of day where nothing dried and every surface felt just a little too close to the skin.

The DVD case still sat on the side table. She didn't reach for it — not yet — but she glanced at it with the kind of fondness that made her throat catch a little.

It was strange how something so simple could change the shape of a place. A voice. A laugh. The sound of screen doors in the background and kids hollering in the yard. It had stitched something back together she hadn't realized was frayed.

She ran her hand across the console, fingertips catching a thin film of dust. Funny how memory gathers, too.

She let the thought pass.

Back at the counter, she remembered she was almost out of coffee. One scoop left, maybe two if she stretched it. She made a mental note to add it to the grocery list, then thought better of it and wrote it down. Lately, if it didn't go down on paper, it slipped away.

She added coffee to the top of her new list and paused. Below that, she wrote one more thing in smaller print:

Call Margaret.

Not for any reason in particular. Just to hear her voice.

Morgan was rinsing out her mug when her phone buzzed once on the counter.

Ashley

Pool's finally warm enough. You around?

Morgan smiled before she even finished reading it. She dried her hands and thumbed a reply.

Morgan

I'm around. That sounds perfect. What time you want me there?

The three dots blinked, then paused, then blinked again.

Ashley

As soon as you can.

Morgan glanced at the time. Still early.

Morgan

Give me just a bit to finish up here. What should I bring?

Ashley

Just yourself. Maybe some tunes? I already iced up the cooler and filled it with your favorite.

Morgan

Sounds good :)

She didn't rush. Finished her coffee, made the bed, pulled on her suit, a cotton T-shirt, and cutoff sweatshorts she wore on beach days.

She tossed in a towel, her phone, and the Bluetooth speaker from the shelf. Fully charged.

The truck was already hot when she climbed in. She rolled the windows down and let the wind do what it could, hair lifting off her shoulders as she turned toward the old road.

The air shimmered above the asphalt, that wavering mirage heat she'd watched as a kid, always certain the road itself was breathing.

Morgan parked under the carport and cut the engine. The heat rushed in the second the A/C quit, but she didn't mind. It felt like summer used to — thick and full of slow down.

She grabbed her bag and walked around back.

Ashley was already in the pool, floating lazily on a blue raft, one arm draped in the water. A cooler sat on the edge of the deck beside a pair of sunglasses and a half-empty bottle of sunscreen.

Ashley lifted her head. "Perfect timing."

Morgan smiled. "Water warm?"

"Eh, warm enough," Ashley said, paddling a slow circle. "Come on in."

Morgan dropped her bag and kicked off her sandals.

The water was a bit cooler than she expected, but in a good way — smooth against her skin and clean-smelling, like the garden hose and sunlight. She dipped under once, then surfaced with her hair slicked back and her shoulders gleaming.

Ashley had drifted toward the deep end, propped on her elbows at the edge of the raft. "Not bad, right?"

Morgan pushed off the wall and floated closer. "Honestly? Feels amazing. Seems summer decided to move in all in one night."

They stayed like that for a while — arms trailing, the occasional soft kick. The sun filtered through the branches overhead, and somewhere across the yard, cicadas had started up.

Ashley reached for the cooler without leaving her raft. "I brought cold Bud Light or Raspberry White Claw — take your pick."

Morgan laughed. "That's the most Southern girl dichotomy I've ever heard."

Ashley tossed her a beer. "I like to keep things balanced."

The can was slick with condensation and the leftover lotion from Ashley's hand. Morgan popped the tab and took a long sip before resting her arms along the side of the pool.

"It's nice here," she said. "I mean, I know I've spent half my life here and everything. But today… it just feels really good."

Ashley tilted her head and smiled, quiet for a second. "I know what you mean."

Morgan grabbed the speaker from her bag and paired her phone. "I'm taking requests. Anything special you want to listen to?"

Ashley smiled. "Ohhhh… let me think. We need something easy."

Morgan scrolled up a few spaces, clicked play, and "Sailing" poured out of the speaker like an ocean breeze. Christopher Cross's baritone-tenor. Crisp and smooth.

Ashley smiled. They didn't say anything for a while after that — just the creak of the float and the soft splash of water as one or the other shifted. Morgan leaned back and closed her eyes. The sun was bright on the inside of her lids.

Ashley let her hand trail in the water, drawing lazy circles with one finger.

"So," she said, her voice easy, "was it hard for you to decide to come back?"

Morgan didn't open her eyes right away. The question wasn't sharp. Just a small stone dropped into still water.

She let out a soft breath, turned her head to the side. "It wasn't my first thought, but once Margaret mentioned it, I began to look forward to it."

Ashley didn't press. She just nodded and watched a dragonfly skim across the water before veering off into the trees.

Morgan sat up slowly, arms draped over the pool's edge. "I think I just... ran out of good reasons to stay."

Ashley smiled faintly. "I can understand that."

They sat in the hush that followed, broken only by the faint chime of wind in the screen door.

Morgan reached for her drink. "You ever feel like your life took a shape while you weren't looking? And then one day you see it, and it's not what you meant it to be?"

Ashley looked over, squinting against the sun. "I think everybody does. But not everybody does something about it."

Morgan didn't say anything. She just took another sip and let the quiet settle between them again.

The song shifted — something older now, the soft sway of Fleetwood Mac filling the space around them like memory.

Ashley leaned back with a sigh, eyes closed, lips tilted in a faint smile. "You always had the best playlists. I loved those mix CDs you used to give me. Such good stuff."

Morgan turned her head and watched her for a second.

The sun had climbed higher, and the heat was starting to press down even with the shade from the trees. Morgan dipped under again, slow and quiet this time, then came up beside the raft. She hooked an elbow over the edge, close enough now to feel the drift of Ashley's fingers in the water.

Ashley opened one eye. "Are you missing it?"

Morgan glanced at her. "Miss what?"

"The city. Atlanta. That version of your life."

Morgan didn't answer right away. She watched a single leaf float across the pool's surface.

"Sometimes I think I miss the idea of it. Not the reality. Not the pace. Maybe it was never about where I lived. Just what I did with my time."

Ashley nodded like she understood. "That's the part no one talks about. The version of life we build in our heads."

Morgan smiled softly. "I built a whole city. Turns out I like old cabins with squeaky steps better."

Ashley grinned, tipping her face toward the sun.

Morgan rested her cheek against her arm, suddenly tired in a good way. The kind that didn't come from stress or running, but from being still long enough to feel full.

After a few minutes, Ashley reached toward the cooler again, grabbed a Bud Light, and leaned over to gently touch the cold can to Morgan's nose.

"You're turning pink," she said.

Morgan took it without a word. Their fingers brushed for a half second too long, but neither of them moved away.

The song changed again — a Bossa Nova by Stan Getz and Astrud Gilberto, silky and warm. It filled the silence in the way words never could. Morgan's throat tightened, but she didn't let it show.

Ashley took a slow sip. "You know... this is our first summer together since eighteen."

Morgan looked over, and for just a moment, didn't think about what came next.

"Yeah," she said quietly. "I've missed it."

They stayed in the water until their fingers puckered and the sun shifted west. Morgan wasn't sure how much time had passed, only that it didn't feel wasted. Ashley had drifted back to the shallow end, head tipped back, eyes closed. A quiet stillness hung between them, easy and known.

Eventually, Morgan climbed out, dripping and barefoot, and grabbed a towel from her bag. She sat on the edge of the deck, legs dangling in the pool, toweling off her hair in slow circles.

Ashley floated toward her, arms outstretched like she was riding a current.

"You hungry?"

Morgan looked over her shoulder. "I am. I skipped breakfast."

Ashley hoisted herself out and reached for her own towel. "I've got cold chicken salad inside."

Morgan smiled. "You know my heart."

Ashley laughed as she wrapped the towel around her shoulders. "I know your stomach."

Inside, the air conditioning hit like an icy breath. The kitchen smelled faintly of basil and Coppertone. Morgan leaned against the counter while Ashley pulled out containers from the fridge.

"I'll make us a couple plates," Ashley said, glancing over her shoulder. "Want to eat out back?"

Morgan nodded. "Sure. Unless you want a break from the heat."

Ashley smiled. "Not yet. It feels nice under the umbrella."

Morgan reached for the speaker and cued something softer this time — a little Sam Cooke, low and close. "Cupid... draw back your bow."

Ashley looked back and grinned.

Morgan didn't say anything. She didn't have to.

The chicken salad was exactly the kind Morgan remembered — heavy on the dill, with just enough celery crunch.

A breeze picked up from the marsh, stirring the edge of the tablecloth and lifting Ashley's hair off her neck. She tucked it behind her ear without thinking.

"It's good to see it lived in again," Ashley said. "The Bar. It missed having people."

Morgan smiled. "I think it did, too."

"You ever think you'd be back this long?"

Morgan shook her head. "Not like this. I thought I'd visit. Help clean up. Maybe stay a week or two." She paused. "Didn't expect to want to stay."

Ashley didn't say anything at first. "Well," she said after a moment, "some places are patient. They wait."

Morgan glanced over. "I'm glad it did."

The sun was beginning to dip. Morgan picked up her can and took a sip, letting the moment settle without rushing it.

Then, without turning her head, she asked, "You want to come by tomorrow? I was thinking about having Margaret and the others over to watch the DVD. You're in a couple frames of it."

Ashley didn't answer right away. She just smiled to herself, eyes on the horizon.

"I'll bring the good beer."

For a long time, neither moved. The marsh breathed and the porch creaked softly beneath them, and Morgan felt the kind of quiet that only comes when everything is right where it belongs — at least for now.

Back at the Bar the light faded slow — more gold than fire, more hush than drama. Morgan stood at the kitchen sink, fingertips still slightly pruned from the pool and a faint pink rising along her nose and shoulders.

She took a lukewarm shower and changed into the softest thing she owned — an old tank top and threadbare shorts.

Back in the kitchen, she poured a glass of water and leaned against the counter. The porch was quiet now. No music, no fan. Just the hum of crickets and the last streaks of pink dragging low across the trees. The cabin was cool, and so were the sheets as she climbed into bed.

Her phone buzzed once. She turned it over and smiled.

Ashley

Loved today. Sweet dreams, M.

Morgan

I did too. Night, Ash.

CHAPTER 24

A Sunday Kind of Love

Morgan lit the grill just after five. The sun was still high, but the heat on the porch was already clinging to the walls, thick and unrelenting. No sense turning on the oven. She'd picked up ribs and a bag of charcoal that morning, along with a container of homemade slaw from Truluck's. Jimmy was bringing chips and ice. Jenn promised corn on the cob. Ashley had offered to bring beer — "the good kind," she'd said, which Morgan knew meant in the bottle and not the can — and a peach cobbler she'd picked up from Mrs. Gertrude's stand off Route 9.

The dinner table was already wiped down and set with mismatched plates and silverware. Morgan had filled a pitcher with sweet tea and floating lemon slices. She moved slowly through the prep, not rushing anything. The music from the living room was low and bluesy — a record she'd cued up earlier and left turning in the background.

It wasn't a special occasion, not really. But something about it felt like it could be.

Like they were gathering around something that wanted to be remembered.

She'd invited them initially to share the DVD — a text thread then grew into a full evening. She just wanted people around. Wanted to see everyone laugh and eat and lean back in their chairs like they had a thousand times before.

She checked the fire, adjusted the ribs on the grate, and leaned against the porch rail for a minute. The sun was angling lower now, catching the tops of the pines and leaving the marsh in gold.

The air felt charged — the quiet before a story changed direction.

The screen door creaked once, and Morgan turned to see Aunt Margaret walking up the steps, arms full of a casserole dish wrapped in a towel.

"You're early," Morgan called.

"I'm a southern lady," Margaret replied. "We show up early, bring too much food and not quite enough gossip; that's why we have to pick more up as we go."

Morgan smiled and stepped forward to help her with the dish.

"Who all's coming?" Aunt Margaret asked, stepping inside to place the dish on the counter.

"The cousins," Morgan said. "And Ash."

"You look nice with your hair down," Margaret said offhandedly, turning back toward the porch. "It's longer than you ever had it, I believe."

Morgan tucked it behind one ear, suddenly self-conscious. "I guess I stopped doing much to it."

Margaret smiled but didn't say more. Instead, she took a seat on the porch bench and looked out at the shifting light.

She stepped back inside just as she heard gravel crunch under tires — Jimmy pulling in.

Jim came through the kitchen door without knocking, a bag of ice in one arm and a case of beer in the other. "Delivery," he said, then leaned into a dramatic stage whisper. "I brought Ash, too."

Morgan's stomach did a small, involuntary turn, but she kept her face even as Ashley followed him in, her arms full of a brown paper bag and a glass pie dish wrapped in foil.

"Hope it's still warm," Ashley said. "Sorry. Running late."

"You're perfect," Morgan said, then caught herself. "I mean — on time. Perfectly on time."

Ashley gave her a quick smile as she moved past into the kitchen.

Jimmy set the ice in the cooler and popped open a beer.

The house was beginning to fill — Jenn and Pete arrived a few minutes later, loud and laughing, arms full of covered dishes. Jenn pressed a kiss to Morgan's cheek then headed straight for the couch like she owned it.

Morgan watched it all unfold — the voices, the clinking dishes, the late-afternoon light stretching long across the floorboards — and let it settle over her. This was what she'd missed. Not the town, exactly. Not the place itself. But the way people who loved you knew how to show up without being asked twice.

The ribs were almost done. She checked them once more, then waved Jimmy over to help carry everything in to the table. Someone put on a record — Etta James, soft and syrupy — and the meal began in that slow, Southern way: one plate at a time, no rush, no plan.

The food was excellent, the stories were better, and for a while, the past felt like something they all agreed to keep quiet just a little longer.

The laughter was easy, but it carried edges — small pauses between jokes, like everyone knew not to name the thing they all felt coming.

Inside, the air-conditioning was holding its own. Morgan had turned it on earlier in the afternoon, and the hum of the old unit was steady in the background. It wasn't cold, exactly, but it was cooler than the porch — and no one complained.

The conversation drifted from stories about Granddad to whether anyone still used the boat landing down by the cut-through. Pete claimed he saw a gator there once, which led to a loud debate about how big it really was and whether or not he'd made it up entirely.

Ashley sat across from Morgan, laughing, chin resting on her hand. The room felt soft around the edges, lit in that in-between way the house always carried just before dusk. Morgan let herself breathe it in — the food, the voices, the comfort of being surrounded by people who'd known her forever.

At some point, the conversation dipped, like it always did after second helpings. Morgan stood up and cleared her throat lightly.

She walked over to the old DVD player and picked up the slim case from the shelf.

"Aunt Margaret, this is the DVD that Abigail made for us from back when we were kids. Jimmy and I watched a little of it already."

Jimmy nodded. "It's my birthday party. It's... kinda wild to see."

Margaret leaned forward slightly, a smile just beginning to rise.

Morgan popped the disc into the tray. "We thought it might be nice to share it."

She clicked play and the screen flickered to life. The room leaned in — faces softening as the first images rolled across the TV. The Bar looked younger. So did they.

Laughter came easy — Pete pointing out his terrible haircut, Jenn groaning at her outfit. Jimmy sat back in his chair, watching himself run wild across the lawn like he was seeing a ghost. He missed those young knees. Morgan saw herself whispering to a seven-year-old Ashley. Some seven-year-old's secret.

Morgan stayed quiet, letting the moment settle around her. She wasn't watching the screen so much as the people. The way they responded. The way it felt to have them here.

Then Granddad's voice came through — off-camera, steady and familiar. A few people chuckled. Someone made a joke. The tape rolled on. Just before the camera panned away, Granddad looked right at it — at them — and smiled.

Margaret didn't move.

Her hands were still, her face unreadable. But something in the stillness lingered. A pause so subtle, it would've gone unnoticed by anyone.

Morgan caught it, though — that small tightening of her aunt's jaw, the way her fingers curled once against her knee before she steadied them again.

She didn't speak. Didn't turn. Just sat there, watching the past ripple across the screen.

And whatever she thought about it, she kept to herself.

When the screen went black, no one moved right away.

There were no credits, no music — just the soft hum of the DVD player and the hush that follows something unexpectedly tender. A few chairs shifted. Someone cleared a throat. But mostly, they sat with it — the old sounds, the bright clothes, the way everything looked so simple through a grainy lens.

Jimmy stood first, stretching and balancing his plate in one hand. "Well," he said, "that was a time capsule."

"Thank you for sharing that," Jenn added, her voice soft. "Really."

Morgan nodded. "Abigail found it. She's the one whc made copies. It belongs to all of us."

"I'm glad she did," Aunt Margaret said.

Ashley helped gather the dishes, moving easily through the space. She passed behind Morgan's chair and touched her shoulder — a small thing, steadying in its own way.

The kitchen filled with the quiet clatter of plates and running water. Pete offered to take out the trash and disappeared through the screen door, muttering something about mosquitoes and the smell of ribs on his shirt.

Morgan rinsed out the tea pitcher, standing at the sink. Outside, the light was beginning to change — that long stretch of golden before the day folds in.

Behind her, Margaret sat at the table, thumbing through the photo envelopes that had come in the box. Nothing urgent in her movements. No sign of the weight she was now carrying. Just a thought she wasn't ready to speak aloud.

Not yet.

The room held its breath with her — a silence that felt alive.

As the sun dipped lower, the house shifted into that softer version of itself — shoes kicked off, chairs turned toward conversation instead of dinner. Someone put on another record, something with a slow sway to it.

Jimmy had stretched out on the couch, Jenn curled into the corner chair with a second helping of cobbler. Morgan smiled, letting the rhythm of it all settle deep in her chest.

Ashley came over with two beers and handed one off without a word.

Morgan took it and tipped the neck toward her. "Thanks."

They stood near the doorway, shoulder to shoulder, watching the others move through the room like it had always been this way — like nobody had ever left or lost or broken a damn thing.

"I haven't seen Margaret sit that still in ten years," Ashley said quietly.

"She's probably just full," Morgan replied, but she knew better.

Ashley looked over, searching a moment. "You okay?"

Morgan hesitated. "Yeah. I'm good."

Ashley looked over, held her gaze a second longer than necessary. "It was a great night."

Morgan nodded. "It was."

She didn't say what she was thinking — that it felt like the kind of night people remember later, without knowing why.

And for a moment, she let herself believe it — that this could be ordinary, that she could stand here with Ashley and feel like the world wasn't holding its breath for something else.

CHAPTER 25

Isn't it pretty to think so?

The next morning came dim and overcast. Not stormy, but thick with that Low Country heaviness that made the sky feel close.

Morgan was halfway through her second cup of coffee when her phone buzzed on the counter.

Margaret

Hon, come by today if you've got time. Just wanted to chat a bit about something. I've been thinking this morning.

It wasn't urgent. But it wasn't nothing, either.

By ten, Morgan was in the truck, heading across town with the radio low and her thoughts even lower. She hadn't asked what Margaret wanted; figured she'd find out soon enough. Aunt Margaret was the opposite of "beat around the bush." If she wanted a sit-down, it meant something.

Margaret was already in her sunroom when Morgan pulled up, looking out toward the road like she'd been expecting her.

"There she is," she said. "Before noon, too."

"Why does everyone say that about me?" Morgan laughed "I haven't slept past noon since college."

Morgan stepped out, T-shirt sleeves rolled up to her shoulders, hair pulled back in a loose twist.

Inside, the house smelled like linen and lemon polish — familiar. Margaret moved through the kitchen with her same quiet rhythm. Morgan took her usual seat at the table — the one she'd eaten dinner in for most of her childhood.

Margaret didn't ease into it. She never did.

"I've been thinking about that video," she said, placing a mug in front of Morgan.

Morgan nodded slowly. "Yeah. I've been thinking about it too. I need to do something nice for Abigail for sharing it. She's very sweet."

"Well, yes, we should. But that's not what I was thinking about." Margaret eased into her own chair. "Morgan, Dad told me specifically not to plan a big party for your tenth birthday. Said it was a special one. He was insistent it just be small, private. I didn't think anything of it at the time."

Morgan sat with that a moment, something clicking.

"Aunt Margaret, the last time I spoke to Mr. Truluck, he mentioned Granddad had come to sit with him and said he couldn't wait to see the smile on my face on my birthday. I thought maybe he was misremembering. He rambled a bit."

Margaret's brow furrowed like she was working out a puzzle. "It's just not making sense to me.

Why would someone who was looking forward to something that deeply... choose to end it all?

"I noticed the timestamp on the DVD yesterday," Margaret said. "It was Jimmy's birthday. February 12th. Dad said he was taking something for repair a week from Friday. That would've been right around the time it happened. Two Fridays later."

Morgan's thoughts scattered, trying to fit the pieces into place.

"Aunt Margaret... there was something in that box from the coroner. The one in the hall closet."

Margaret leaned in.

"A note Granddad made... '$80 noless.'"

Morgan grabbed a napkin and pencil and wrote it out to show her.

"At first, we thought it was about a sale — maybe something he was fixing up. Then Jimmy remembered Knowles Armory. We figured it was a note to himself that he scratched out. noless = Knowles."

The house creaked softly, as if listening. The wall clock ticked off the seconds like a metronome.

Margaret spoke again, her voice low. "Let's keep this between us for now. I'm going to speak with John Murphy at the coroner's office. Ask a few questions. It can't hurt."

"I agree," Morgan said. "It can't hurt to ask. And I'll keep it to myself."

Outside, a breeze stirred the trees, and the light shifted — subtle, but real.

Morgan took out her phone. A message from Claire was still sitting unread from the night before. She looked at it, then at Margaret.

"I'm not going back," she said. "Not to Atlanta. At least not anytime soon."

Margaret didn't smile, but she didn't look surprised. She just lifted her mug, took a small sip, and said, "Good."

Morgan exhaled slowly and leaned back, letting the weight of the morning settle.

Margaret folded her hands. "I wonder what he had planned for your birthday."

Morgan nodded. "Sometimes it's not about the answer. Just knowing somebody was thinking of you... that's enough."

They sat like that for a while. Not filling the space. Just letting it be.

When Morgan finally stood to leave, Margaret walked her out.

"Thanks for calling me," Morgan said, hugging her. "For sharing this with me."

Back in the truck, she rested her hand on the gearshift but didn't turn the key right away. The sky was still overcast, but the air felt clearer — like something had broken open and let in light.

The Bar smelled like wood and weather... and something else. The low, lingering scent of cigar smoke that hadn't been there when she left.

Morgan paused inside the screen door.

It wasn't sharp. Not strong. Barely there.

Present.

Like someone had passed through and left a trace.

She didn't move. The air felt still, expectant. The chair in the corner was empty. The needle on the turntable rested in its cradle.

She stepped inside. Her thoughts were still at Margaret's table — not just what had been said, but how she said it. Like she'd been holding something in her hand for years and had finally opened her fingers.

The light cut gold and low across the porch.

The scent was gone.

Still, Morgan glanced toward the hallway — toward the closet door that always seemed to shift no matter how many times she latched it.

It hadn't moved.

Not yet.

She stepped to the sink, sipped from the glass of water she'd left there, and braced her hands against the counter.

Something was building.

Not heavy. Not ominous.

Close.

She didn't turn on any music. The house already had its own — cicadas in the trees, the faint creak of the porch settling into evening.

She walked toward the hallway and paused.

The door stayed shut.

She reached for the latch.

Stopped herself.

Leaning in slightly, she listened.

The silence wasn't empty. It felt aware — like the space between a question and its answer.

She stepped away without touching it.

The wind brushed across the porch and nudged the screen door with a soft rattle.

She looked up.

The scent was back. Faint. Dry. Tobacco and something older — wood polish, maybe. Leather.

She didn't get up. Didn't scan the room.

Just whispered, "Hey."

The smoke thinned, then disappeared.

Morgan sat with her notebook but didn't open it. The air was still forgiving — still early enough to write, late enough to think.

She pulled her knees up into the chair and looked toward the hallway.

Still shut.

Still waiting.

The conversation had left more in its wake than she expected. Not dramatic. Not even clear. But something had shifted.

She flipped back to her last entry. One line stopped her:

Maybe it's not about solving the mystery. Maybe it's about giving it space to tell its own story.

She hadn't remembered writing it.

But it felt true.

She wrote beneath it:

What if he didn't mean to leave.

No floodgates opened. No cascade of insight.

Just that.

Whole. Uncomplicated.

She closed the notebook, reached up to the cabinet above the fridge, and turned out the light.

That night she dreamed of the river.

Not the day it happened. Not the days after.

Just the water — smooth and slow. Pale green where the sun caught it, dark beneath the overhangs.

The old aluminum boat drifting near the bank. No motor. No sound. Just a paddle resting on the bench seat.

Empty.

In the dream, she stood on the bank, watching. Not calling. Not moving.

And beside her — though no one touched her — was the unmistakable feeling of someone there.

Like an invisible hand on her back.

Morgan sat up too fast. The Jim Beam in her system made it feel like her soul took a second to catch up to her body.

The morning light was blue and thin. The air in the room felt untouched — cool, weightless.

She rubbed her eyes, crossed the room barefoot, and started the coffee.

And then — soft at first, then clearer — came the unmistakable sound of that muffled music. Cash..

"*Well, I woke up Sunday mornin' / With no way to hold my head that didn't hurt. And the beer I had for breakfast wasn't bad / So I had one more for dessert.*"

Morgan let out a dry laugh.

"Your sarcasm is not lost on me, I'll have you know," she muttered aloud in the general direction of the HiFi.

She poured her coffee and stepped onto the porch.

The marsh was quiet. Not still. Just right.

She sat on the top step, mug in hand, watching the birds in the grass. Listening.

The dream hadn't been a memory.

But it mattered.

CHAPTER 26

The road was dusty and well-travelled

The morning passed slowly, thick with that unsettled quiet that sometimes followed clarity. Morgan didn't write. She didn't clean. She folded a load of laundry she'd forgotten in the dryer, then sat for a long time at the kitchen table, flipping through a notebook without really reading.

Outside, the marsh was a pale blur of green and gold, but the air had turned. Not stormy. Not yet. Just heavier than usual — the coast always knew something was coming before the forecast did.

Her phone buzzed around nine.

Ashley

Hey — random ask. Want to ride to Columbia with me? Picking up some empty sandbags for the store and a couple other thing ahead of this storm getting any bigger. You'd be good company.

Morgan stared at the message for a beat.

She hadn't planned on doing anything today. But she didn't want to be alone either — not with the thoughts she had, not with the kind of air that made everything feel like it was waiting. She typed back.

Morgan

Sure. What time?

Ashley's reply came quick:

Ashley

Leaving around 10:30. Taking the store truck. Meet you there.

Morgan's heart beat a little faster, though she couldn't have said why.

She went to change — jeans, a black tee, hair pulled back into something almost tidy — then paused before walking out the door.

For a second, she thought she smelled it again.

Cigar smoke. Dry and faint.

She turned, but the chair was still. The house was quiet.

She let the screen door shut gently behind her. The ride up felt easier than Morgan expected.

Ashley drove with one hand on the wheel, windows down, radio low playing faintly through the cracked speakers. Morgan rested her elbow on the edge of the open window, letting the wind tangle her hair as the road unfurled ahead of them in long, empty stretches.

They didn't talk much at first. Just the steady hum of tires, the occasional note of guitar. But it wasn't awkward. It felt like driving with someone you knew like the back of your hand. The silence was a comfort.

They passed an old fruit stand that had long closed. The paint on the sign had peeled unrecognizably. A hawk circled above the field behind it.

Morgan smiled faintly. "Granddad used to make me name every bird we passed on this road."

Ashley smiled and said "He once told me I'd never get a husband if I couldn't bait a hook."

Morgan laughed out loud. "Did you ever learn?"

Ashley looked over at her, eyes bright as she turned up a favorite tune on the radio. "I did learn, but not for the prize of a husband."

"You know I saved every single mix CD you ever made me?"

"Are you serious?"

"Yep. Saved them all.

The truck rolled on in silence for a beat too long. Morgan shifted, just slightly, but didn't say anything.

Ashley glanced at her, voice quieter now. "You want to listen to one?"

Morgan laughed. "You have them with you?"

Ashley reached behind the seat at the next red light and pulled out an old CD case — the kind with cracked plastic sleeves and faded Sharpie scrawls. She flipped through like it was muscle memory, her fingers pausing on one labeled "Morgan Mix #3 – Spring '03."

She slid it into the truck's CD player. The stereo clicked, whirred — and then a low guitar line came through the speakers, scratchy and uneven. James Taylor, sure enough. The first few seconds cut out, then the song found its footing.

"In my mind I'm gone to Carolina..."

Morgan looked out the window. Her throat tightened without warning.

"I used to play this on repeat that spring," she said. "That was the year I almost didn't come back from break."

Ashley nodded, slow. "I remember."

The road stretched quiet ahead of them, lined with billboards sun-faded to ghostly colors.

Morgan turned to her. "Why'd you keep them?"

Ashley didn't answer right away. She just kept her eyes on the road, one hand resting soft on the gearshift.

"Because you have really good taste in music," she said finally.

"And because it made it feel like you were still here."

Morgan blinked, but tears didn't fall.

She let the music play. Let the words settle. Let the moment stretch wide between them, not empty — just waiting to be filled.

They made it to Columbia by early afternoon. The drive had been quiet after the music started. Ashley drove with one hand, steady and sure, like she'd been taking this route for years.

They picked up the pallets of empty sandbags from a supply warehouse just outside the city, then swung by a local hardware distributor Ashley liked. Morgan helped load heavy-duty plastic bins, first-aid kits, and plastic flashlights into the truck bed.

"You really think you'll need all this?" Morgan asked, brushing her hands off on her jeans.

"Probably not," Ashley said. "But if we do, I'd rather be the one who had too much than the one who ran out."

Morgan nodded. That made sense. It always had, the way Ashley planned for things. Even when they were younger — when Morgan had written essays the night before they were due — Ashley had started hers the day they were assigned. She always said she didn't like rushing.

Once the errands were done, Ashley suggested lunch. They ended up at a tiny place off a side road — one of those Southern diners that hadn't been remodeled since its grand opening in the '60s. The server called them both "sugar," and the catfish special came with two sides and sweet tea.

Morgan watched Ashley as they ate. There was something unhurried in the way she sat, like she wasn't in a rush to be anywhere else.

"I missed this," Morgan said finally. "Not just the food. Just spending time."

Ashley looked up from her fork. "Me too."

Morgan held her gaze.

Whatever this was — it wasn't nothing. It wasn't a weekly brunch date with an old school friend.

The clouds thickened on the way home, and the road began to darken at the edges.

Ashley reached forward and turned the radio down.

"You okay?"

Morgan nodded, slow. "Yeah. Just thinking."

She didn't say what about.

Ashley didn't press. She just kept driving, her fingers steady on the wheel, like she already knew.

They got back just before five.

A couple of the store's part-time guys were already waiting out front, ready to unload. Ashley eased the truck into place and killed the engine. Neither of them moved at first.

"You want me to help?" Morgan asked, thumb hooked in her pocket.

Ashley shook her head. "Nah. They've got it."

Morgan nodded, then hesitated.

Ashley opened the door, but before she could climb out, Morgan spoke.

"What are you doing for dinner tomorrow night?"

Ashley turned to look at her, one hand still on the handle.

Morgan tried to keep her voice steady. "I was thinking about cooking. It's been a while since I really spent time in the kitchen. Would you like to come to dinner?"

Ashley's mouth curved into the smallest smile — not surprised, not smug. Just something warm that made Morgan's chest tighten a little.

"I'd like that," she said.

Morgan nodded. "Cool."

Ashley hopped out, calling a quick thanks to the guys already pulling the first tarp loose. Morgan stayed where she was for a moment longer, watching the afternoon light stretch across the sidewalk.

She didn't know exactly what tomorrow would be, but she was looking forward to it.

CHAPTER 27

Minute By Minute

Morgan stood at the kitchen window with her coffee, watching mist lift off the yard in thin, rising trails. The trees were slick with leftover rain, darker than usual, and the air coming through the screen door was surprisingly cool.

She crossed the room and tapped her phone, scrolling just far enough to find the old playlist she used to put on when she cooked. A moment later, "Minute by Minute" eased out through the Bluetooth speaker — Michael McDonald's voice warm, patient, a steady hum beneath the quiet.

She took her coffee to the porch and stood at the railing. Her feet were bare, the wood cool against her skin. A few birds rustled in the brush beyond the clearing, and the reeds by the water stirred just enough to shimmer. She didn't feel restless. But she felt... ready.

Back inside, she rinsed her cup, then reached for her phone. Not to scroll. Just to send one thing.

Morgan

Hey. Do you like grilled salmon?

Ashley replied fast.

Ashley

Love it. Want me to bring anything?

Morgan

Nope... it's all covered

Morgan smiled and slipped the phone into her back pocket.

It had been a long time since she cooked for someone. Really cooked. Not boiled noodles and sauce from a jar. Not scrambled eggs at midnight. Real food. Thoughtful food.

She opened the fridge and looked inside like she might already have what she needed. She didn't.

She grabbed her keys and made a list in her head as she pulled on her boots. Cedar planks. Fresh salmon. Soy sauce and brown sugar for a marinade. Asparagus. Lemon. Maybe something for dessert. And wine. Definitely wine.

Truluck's wouldn't cut it and neither would the main grocery store in town. She'd need to drive to the next big city over — she knew exactly where to go.

Today Morgan didn't rush. Driving these back roads was becoming more enjoyable. The sky above was a steady pale blue now, streaked with leftover clouds that didn't seem in a hurry to go anywhere.

The city wasn't far — twenty-five minutes if she took the old road, which she always did. She liked how the landscape opened up once she passed the last bend of trees.

There was a hardware store up ahead she remembered from years ago, and behind it, the small garden center where Granddad used to pick up bags of mulch and seed potatoes in spring. She parked beneath a crooked live oak and stepped out, list still forming in her head.

Inside, the store hadn't changed much. Dusty in the corners. Pegboards hung with tools in no particular order. The man behind the counter gave her a nod and didn't ask questions.

She found the cedar planks on a back shelf, packed in plastic but still smelling faintly of wood smoke.

By the time she walked out, the sun had climbed higher. Warm, but not too much. A good day for cooking outside.

At the grocery store, she wandered a little — not aimlessly, but slowly. She picked through the produce like she was choosing paint swatches, taking her time with each bundle. She wanted asparagus, yes, but only if it snapped clean. She wanted tomatoes firm but not pale. A lemon that felt heavy in her hand.

The salmon was fresh — flown in from somewhere far off, but a beautiful shade of pink. The man behind the counter wrapped it in thick white paper and handed it over with a nod like he approved of her choices.

She lingered in the wine section longer than she meant to. Something dry. Something simple. It didn't need to impress — just to go well with the food.

Before checkout, she added a small carton of vanilla ice cream and a small, dark chocolate flourless cake she hadn't planned on. Something about them felt right.

By the time she got back to The Bar, it was mid-afternoon and the sun had pushed any remaining clouds out to the edge of the sky.

The cedar planks went into a dish of water to soak. She turned the speaker back on, thumbed through her phone, and let a jazz station play for a while — piano, upright bass, something smoky and low.

The salmon stayed in the fridge, still wrapped. The vegetables sat on the counter beside the cutting board.

She poured a glass of wine and sat with it for a few minutes before doing anything else. It felt good to take her time.

She started with the vegetables. Not the fast way — not rough-chopped and dumped in a pan — but the kind of careful slicing that felt like its own kind of meditation. The asparagus got trimmed at an angle, the tomatoes halved and sprinkled with sea salt to rest. She set a skillet on the stove with a splash of olive oil and added a few sprigs of thyme just to warm the air.

Once the cedar planks had soaked long enough not to burn, she dried them with a towel and set one on the counter. The salmon went skin-side down, seasoned with lemon zest, cracked pepper and a brushing of soy and sugar.

When she lit the grill, the flame caught quick. The hiss of heat meeting water-soaked wood was immediate — sharp, then soft. She placed the planks on the rack and closed the lid.

Back inside, the kitchen began to smell like something real. Like dinner in progress. The kind that promised warmth and good conversation.

She took another sip of wine, then pulled out two linen napkins from the far drawer — ones she hadn't used since before she moved back.

The music shifted again. Not a song she recognized, but something in a major key — a little playful, a little blue. It was good enough. She smiled and got back to work.

She set the table while the salmon finished — nothing formal, just two plates, the linen napkins, and silverware laid neatly beside them. The wine glasses weren't crystal, but they caught the light the way she remembered.

In the kitchen, she checked the vegetables. They'd softened just enough in the skillet, taking on a light char from the pan and the thyme. She transferred them to a low dish, squeezing a bit of lemon juice over top.

Out back, the cedar plank had started to darken around the edges. The salmon glistened. Beautifully mahogany colored by the salty sweet marinade, edges curling slightly, the scent of thyme and woodsmoke drifting across the yard. She lifted the lid and checked it once — just to be sure — then closed it again.

Back inside, she looked around. Everything was ready. And for a moment, she stood still, wiping her hands on a dish towel and listening to the quiet jazz spilling softly from the speaker.

It didn't feel like waiting.

It felt like welcoming.

Morgan had just pulled the salmon from the grill when she heard the crunch of tires in the gravel. She didn't rush. Just closed the lid and wiped her hands one more time on the dish towel.

The knock was light — more a rhythm than a sound — and when she opened the door, Ashley stood there in jeans and a white T-shirt. Her hair was still damp from a shower.

When she stepped inside, she paused, looking around. "Morgan, it smells amazing in here."

"Good! That was the goal." Morgan smiled.

Ashley followed her into the kitchen and leaned in to peek at the plated vegetables. "Okay, you're showing off."

Morgan poured her a glass of wine without asking, handed it over. "Not showing off. Just… enjoying myself."

They settled at the table, the food between them still steaming.

Morgan served the salmon first — one long fillet, perfectly flaked, lemon slices soft and translucent along the top.

Ashley took her first bite and let her eyes close. "Okay," she said, swallowing. "You're definitely showing off."

Morgan laughed. "That one I'll take."

They didn't rush. The jazz played on behind them, low and steady. Every few minutes, one of them reached for more asparagus or another forkful of tomato. The napkins stayed mostly in their laps. The wine disappeared slowly.

Ashley leaned back in her chair, wine glass cupped in both hands. The grill still crackled faintly out back — the coals not quite dead yet, hissing low in the ash.

Ashley took one last bite and shook her head softly. "This was so good, Morgan."

"I'm glad you liked it," Morgan replied, not quite meeting Ashley's gaze.

Outside, the porch light had started to hum, soft against the gathering dusk.

Ashley stood to clear her plate.

"Let me do that." Morgan reached to stop her. "You're the guest."

Ashley was already at the sink. "Oh no... you did the hard work. I can help clean"

Morgan laughed and stood, gathering her own plate and the salad bowl. "Alright, but I have dessert."

Ashley glanced over her shoulder. "You made dessert?"

Morgan opened the freezer. "Not homemade, but vanilla ice cream and dark chocolate. It counts."

Ashley grinned. "It definitely counts."

They finished the last of the wine with the dishes half-done, hands bumping lightly at the sink while the water ran warm and the night moved in.

Ashley dried as Morgan rinsed, trading quiet smiles and soft laughter. The kind of rhythm that shows up when two people aren't trying to impress each other.

When they were through, Ashley leaned against the counter.

"I forgot all about that old record player until you were using it last week," she said, glancing toward the living room. "It still sounds good!"

Morgan nodded. "It does. I've been listening to Granddad's collection since I got here."

Ashley walked over and crouched down, flipping the power and lifting the lid. She ran her fingers over the spines of the records stacked nearby.

"You got any beach music in here?"

"Oh yeah," Morgan said. "Granddad liked a little bit of everything."

Ashley pulled out a few options, smiling wider when she found one labeled Shag Favorites – Volume 2. "Oh my God. Stagger Lee."

She placed it gently on the platter, set the needle, and turned up the volume just enough to fill the room.

Morgan stepped in from the kitchen, drying her hands on a dish towel.

Ashley grinned and held out her hand.

Morgan didn't hesitate. She took it.

The rhythm was second nature. They fell into step the way they used to on the dock behind Ashley's house, barefoot and sunburned and too young to care about who might be watching.

One song bled into another. "Under the Boardwalk," "Sixty Minute Man," "Carolina Girls." Each one pulling them deeper into memory.

They laughed, twirled each other clumsily in the tight space between the rug and the coffee table.

Ashley caught Morgan's eye during "Be Young, Be Foolish, Be Happy," and mouthed the words dramatically.

Morgan dipped her, just for fun.

They were still laughing when the music stopped.

The silence came just long enough to notice.

Then another track started.

Slower. Muted. Morgan could tell the Bar had chosen the next song.

A piano, low and unhurried. Then a man's voice..

"Don't go changin. To try and please me. You never let me down before.. mmm...mmm..mmm."

They stood there, neither moving, as the song played on. His voice wasn't grand. It didn't try to prove anything. It just offered what it had — and let the rest unfold.

"That's strange, said Ashley. "I didn't put that on."

"Sometimes it switches over to the radio. It's old." replied Morgan. No time to explain right now.

Ashley's eyes stayed on Morgan the whole time.

Morgan looked down at the floor, then back at her.

Ashley stepped closer. Carefully. Slowly.

They met in the middle of the rug, inches apart, neither one making the first move.

Morgan swallowed hard. "Ash, we can change it —"

Ashley reached up and tucked a strand of hair behind Morgan's ear. "I know, but I want to dance with my best friend."

Then, gently, she took Morgan's hand.

"You always have my unspoken passion..."

They didn't dance, not really. Just held each other — a kind of stillness that counted as motion. Like the tides. Like breath.

When the song ended, Ashley didn't let go.

Neither did Morgan.

Ashley placed her hand on Morgan's cheek... wiped away a tear Morgan hadn't realized had fallen.

Morgan leaned in and kissed her — tender, slow, unguarded — her hands at the small of Ashley's back.

Years of memories, heartache, and quiet love wrapped themselves into that one kiss.

Ashley felt it to the bone.

The hum of the old console continued long after all the music stopped.

Morgan rested her forehead against Ashley's and closed her eyes.

The house was still, but alive — every wall recording the sound of something beginning.

CHAPTER 28

Somewhere safe to land

Morgan woke slowly, the pale light of early morning soft across the ceiling. It was that quiet threshold between night and day — the moment the world was still deciding which it wanted to be. The house was still, except for the faint rustle of marsh reeds outside.

Morgan turned her head.

Ashley lay on her side, one hand tucked beneath the pillow, her breath slow and even. Her hair spilled across her back in loose waves, the edge of the sheet slipped low on one shoulder.

Without thinking, Morgan reached to pull it back up — a gesture she had performed probably 100 times from years of sleepovers and campouts. This time, she left a gentle kiss at the curve of Ashley's shoulder blade before slipping out of bed and into the quiet to make coffee.

In the kitchen, Morgan moved carefully, not letting the cabinet doors thud or the mugs clink. She scooped the coffee slowly, measuring by instinct. The scent of the grounds hit first — warm and bitter, familiar — followed by the soft gurgle of the water beginning to heat.

Outside, the marsh was waking up. Pale mist clung to the low places, and a few birds called out across the stillness. A soft breeze moved through the palmettos.

Morgan leaned against the counter, arms folded, watching the pot begin to drip. The quiet was full but not heavy. She could still feel the shape of Ashley's shoulder beneath her lips, the softness of her breathing before she left the room. Nothing about it felt rushed. Just real.

She heard the creak of the bedroom floorboards first, then the soft pad of bare feet.

Ashley appeared in the doorway; hair tousled. She blinked once at the morning light, then crossed the room without a word.

Morgan didn't turn. She didn't have to.

Ashley stepped in behind her, wrapping her arms around Morgan and resting her cheek against her back. Her skin was warm and still kissed with sleep.

Morgan didn't speak. She just reached up and gently laid one hand over Ashley's forearm — anchoring her there, steady and sure.

"Mmm. Coffee," Ashley murmured, voice low and rough at the edges.

Morgan smiled, closing her eyes for a moment, letting herself lean back into the weight of her. "Already poured you some."

Ashley didn't move. "Just want this part for a second."

Morgan let the quiet stretch, her hand resting over Ashley's. Neither of them needed to say anything more.

When Ashley peeled away, she brushed past Morgan's shoulder and moved to the table, folding into one of the chairs with a sleepy ease, like the rhythm of the morning had always included this.

Morgan set the coffee down in front of her without a word. Ashley gave her a soft, grateful look as her fingers wrapped around the warm mug.

Morgan sat across from her.

Ashley looked up at her over the rim of her cup.

"Did you sleep okay?"

Morgan nodded. "I did."

Ashley gave a small smile. "Better than I have in a long time."

The quiet settled between them again, companionable now, touched with the hum of the morning coming to life. A bird called once from the edge of the marsh. Somewhere distant, a truck passed on the highway.

Ashley set her mug down and rubbed a hand across her face. "I should probably head home. I've got to open up the store."

Morgan nodded. "Want to take a shower here?"

Ashley shook her head gently. "I've got what I need at the house. But I'll be back later — if that's alright."

Morgan just looked at her, a smile playing faintly at the corners of her mouth. "Of course."

A soft buzz broke the moment — Morgan's phone on the counter. She picked it up and glanced at the screen.

Weather alert: Tropical system expected to strengthen. Coastal watches possible.

Ashley noticed the shift in her expression. "Everything okay?"

Morgan turned the screen toward her. "Storm's picking up speed. They might post watches soon."

Ashley reached for her cup again, frowning just slightly. "Well... this place has made it through some tough storms. I think it can get through another."

Morgan looked out the window toward the marsh and the thin trees lining the back of the property.

"Yeah," she said softly. "I guess we'll see."

Ashley stood, taking her empty mug to the sink and rinsing it.

"I'll be back before dinner," she said, glancing toward the door. "Do you need anything from town?"

Morgan shook her head. "Think I'm set. Just gonna do some work I've been putting off."

She didn't say writing. She didn't have to.

Morgan stepped forward and kissed her — not rushed, not hesitant — just a simple, sure press of lips that felt like punctuation.

Ashley exhaled when they pulled apart. "Okay then," she said, smiling as she finally stepped out onto the porch.

"See you soon."

Morgan watched her go, the screen door easing shut behind her.

She lingered a moment in the whisper of wind and bird calls, then turned back and crossed to the kitchen counter to set down her mug. The room felt a little too big, a little too still, without Ashley here — but not empty. Just wide with potential.

She checked her phone. The alert for the storm hung in the notifications pane, a low rumble at the edge of her awareness. Not yet urgent, but close enough to matter.

Morgan set her coffee beside it and drew in a slow breath. She didn't mind the storm — it felt right, somehow. Needed, even. A hunkering down. A cleansing. And perhaps, a turning.

She moved to the window and looked out through the screen at the marsh. The reeds, still heavy with dew, caught the golden mid-morning light. In her chest, something untangled.

With a single, decisive motion, she picked up her notebook from the counter and flipped to the next blank page. She uncapped her favorite pen and let the ink settle, steady as the tide.

She pressed the tip to paper and wrote:

Sometimes, a storm is the only way to start again.

She paused, then added a date.

Maybe it was the writing. Maybe it was the possible hurricane. Maybe it was Ashley.

Morgan took a measured sip of coffee and smiled softly at herself. Then she pocketed the phone with the alert still blinking.

Whatever was brewing — in weather, in heart, in home — she was ready.

CHAPTER 29

A storm was coming, but it hadn't come yet

Morgan wrote until the light changed.

At first, the pages came slowly, but then something loosened. The lines began to stretch and find their rhythm. By noon, she had filled several pages — not with anything she planned to keep, but with something closer to breath. She didn't question it. She just let the pen keep moving.

Outside, the breeze had picked up. The wind slipped around the eaves, creating a low, uncertain music.

Morgan sat back and stretched her arms overhead. Her coffee had gone cold hours ago, and her body was beginning to feel the ache of being still too long. She rose, walked to the sink, and poured the rest down the drain. The sky had shifted — clouds higher now, moving faster, trailing thin shadows across the marsh.

She grabbed her phone and thumbed it awake.

The same alert was still pinned to the top:

Tropical System Expected to Strengthen — Watches Possible by Morning.

Morgan didn't feel panicked. But there was a buzz under her skin now — the same one she'd felt as a kid when the weather changed, that moment before a thunderstorm when the light turned silver and the trees all leaned in the same direction.

She opened the screen door and stepped out barefoot onto the porch. The wind had a taste to it now. Saltier.

Morgan stood there a long time, watching the trees sway, one hand resting lightly on the post. She hadn't heard from Ashley yet — but she imagined the store was busier than usual. She'd text her in a bit.

She stepped back inside and let the screen door ease shut behind her. She glanced at the notebook still open on the table, but she wasn't ready to sit again.

Instead, she moved through the house, gathering up a few stray items, folding a blanket that had slipped off the back of the couch — the kind of light cleaning that wasn't about tidying so much as giving her hands and mind something to do.

By the time she reached the bedroom, the breeze had grown stronger, the windows humming in their panes. It would be like this for a day or two before things turned. Morgan smoothed the sheets, lifted the pillow that still carried the faint scent of Ashley's shampoo and perfume. It took her back to the night before. She closed her eyes and smiled.

Her phone buzzed again.

This time, it was a text.

Ashley

OMG. Busy day. The town gets crazier every year once the first weather warnings start.

The guys are coming out later this afternoon with sandbags, and I'll be out that way after I close up.

Morgan smiled faintly at the screen and typed back:

Morgan

I'm sorry. I figured today might be crazy for you. You're amazing! Thank you!

A few seconds later, the three little dots bounced once, then disappeared.

Morgan tossed the phone onto the bed and sat beside it. The wind had grown louder now, the palmetto leaves scraping softly against the windowpane.

The afternoon was still ahead of her — but there was something in the air now. A slight tilting. A lean.

She was used to it — the feeling that something was coming.

This time, though, it didn't feel like dread.

It felt like another step of good change.

By late afternoon, the clouds had thickened into a pale ceiling overhead. Not dark yet — not threatening — but layered, like a warning tucked just out of reach.

Morgan wasn't the kind to start prepping too early, but she had done this more than a few times before and knew not to wait too long.

She took a quick inventory of staples she had: extra water, a few cans of soup, a half-bag of charcoal.

She jotted a short list — more out of habit than need — then folded it in half and tucked it under the magnet on the fridge.

Her phone buzzed again. This time, it was another alert.

Tropical Storm Warning Likely by Morning. Prepare for Deteriorating Conditions.

Morgan turned the volume down and pocketed the phone.

She looked around the kitchen — the old fridge humming softly, the faint tick of the wall clock. Outside, a gust of wind rolled through the trees, louder this time.

She heard tires on gravel, then saw a familiar truck turn the corner of the cabin.

Jimmy climbed out slow, one hand hooked on the open window as he leaned in to grab his cap from the dash. He gave her a nod and started up the steps.

"You survivin'?" he asked.

"More or less."

He looked out across the trees, wind pressing through in steady waves now. "Figured I'd stop by. See if you were actually paying attention to the forecast."

Morgan smirked. "Aunt Margaret told you to check on me, didn't she?"

Jimmy nodded. "Yep."

He tipped his chin toward the driveway. "I'm heading into town — Truluck's, maybe a couple other stops. You need anything? You're definitely gonna need sandbags. The river's gonna cover this yard."

She thought for a second. "I've got a few things, but I made a short list. Ashley's having sandbags delivered from the store. I was gonna pick the rest of this stuff up tomorrow."

"And that's why Aunt Margaret told me to swing by today," he said. "There won't be anything left tomorrow. You've spent one too many hurricanes in Atlanta."

Morgan leaned against the doorframe; arms folded. "You being all helpful and prepared is weird. I'm not used to it."

He started back down the steps, waving behind him. "I'll be back in the morning with this stuff. I'll help stack the bags."

Morgan watched him go, the screen door easing shut behind her. For most of their lives, Jimmy had teased her more than he'd helped her — quick with a joke, always on the move. But there was something different in his tone now. Still easy, still him. Just... steadier.

She wasn't used to it. But she didn't mind it.

A few minutes later, she heard the crunch of tires again — slower this time, heavier. A white flatbed truck with Harbor Iron & Tool stenciled on the door came around the bend and eased into the clearing beside the porch. Two guys in worn work shirts climbed out, one of them already unfastening the tie-down straps in back.

"We'll get 'em stacked up for you. Where you want 'em?"

"Right here's fine," she said, nodding to the back wall of the porch. "Thanks, guys."

The bags made soft thuds as the men carried them from the truck and lined them along the porch. The work was efficient, the kind of rhythm born of practice

— one man hauling, the other stacking. Morgan stayed back, out of the way.

The breeze kicked up again, carrying with it the smell of mud and brine. Overhead, the clouds had started to gather more purposefully now — not just a haze, but a thick ceiling of gray that flattened the light across everything.

One of the men wiped his forehead with his sleeve as he dropped the last bag in place. "That should do it."

Morgan stepped inside, grabbed two bottles of water from the fridge and a tip from her wallet, and handed them over.

"Appreciate it," she said, stepping down to meet them. "Y'all be safe."

They climbed back into the truck, the door creaking as it shut behind them. Morgan stood there a moment longer, watching the shape of the bags, how solid they looked against the porch.

She stepped back inside, her hand trailing the doorframe. The living room felt dimmer now, the light flatter, more like late evening than it actually was. She turned on the lamp in the corner and the TV so she could hear what the storm was deciding to do.

She didn't know exactly when Ashley would show up — just that she would. That alone felt warm.

Around six, the sound of a car pulling into the drive pulled Morgan from her thoughts. She stepped out onto the porch and saw Ashley climbing out of her dusty Subaru, a plastic container balanced on her hip and a bag over one shoulder.

"You made it," Morgan said, stepping down to meet her.

"Barely. I swear if one more person had asked me if we still had D batteries, I was gonna lose my mind!" Ashley said, grinning. "Here. I brought a few extra things in case you forgot how to hurricane."

Morgan took the bag from her, laughing. "You and Jimmy both. It's like y'all had a meeting."

Ashley followed her inside and dropped the plastic container on the counter. "That's some leftover potato salad from Mom's place, and I tossed in a couple of flashlights."

She looked at Morgan and grinned. "By the way… do you have any D batteries?"

Morgan smiled back as Ashley kissed her — a laugh still on her lips.

"I'm gonna owe you both a steak dinner when this is over," Morgan said, pulling a carton of eggs from the fridge.

Ashley leaned back against the counter, her arms crossed. "You cooking?"

"Thinking omelets. Want one?"

"Ummm… yes please."

Morgan moved easily around the kitchen, pulling a few things from the fridge and setting them out — bell pepper, cheddar, tomato. Ashley stepped in to slice the vegetables while Morgan cracked the eggs.

They worked in quiet rhythm, the wind starting to knock against the windows with more confidence now. It wasn't loud, just… present.

Over dinner, they talked about nothing — how their days went and the kind of light, shared history that filled the space without needing to be profound.

After they ate, Ashley stacked the plates in the sink and Morgan wiped down the counter, her movements slow and unhurried. The kitchen was warm now — not just from the stove, but from something steady that had settled between them. Easy. Familiar.

Morgan glanced out the window. The light was almost gone, the sky a heavy slate. "You staying?" she asked, not turning around.

Ashley didn't answer right away. She rinsed a plate and set it in the drying rack before drying her hands on the dish towel. "I was hoping to," she said. "If that's okay."

Morgan turned to face her. "Of course it's okay."

They didn't need to say more. The question hadn't been about permission — it was about belonging.

And right now, there was nowhere else either of them wanted to be.

CHAPTER 30

A very fine house

The morning came gray, and wind stirred.

Morgan woke first, the sound of the screen rattling in the window pulling her from sleep. She listened for a bit before she moved. The bedroom felt cooler than usual — the kind of cool that didn't belong in summer — and the light outside was flat and colorless, thick with motion.

Beside her, Ashley slept soundly, her breath slow and even. Morgan let herself lie still a moment longer. It felt like a gift — waking up to this woman. She imagined it always would.

The storm had grown overnight. Stronger. Closer.

She eased out of bed, careful not to wake Ashley, and padded to the kitchen. The house groaned more than usual — like it knew something was on the way.

The TV was still on from the night before. Morgan turned the volume up just enough to hear the anchor confirm it:

"Hurricane Renée is now a strong Category 3. Forecast track steady — expected to make landfall late tonight or early morning near the southern coastline."

She started the coffee, then checked her phone.

A text sent just after midnight:

Jimmy

It's gonna be worse than they thought. Pete and Jenn are at Aunt Margaret's — full house, but they're fine with the generator. I'm staying at The Bar. Just in case. I'll be there for breakfast. Bringing tarps.

Morgan was standing at the sink when she heard Jimmy's truck pull up. She didn't rush to the door — just let it creak open on its own like it always did.

"Coffee?" she asked.

Jimmy stepped inside, brushing a few stray raindrops off his jacket.

He took the mug and a long sip, looked around the kitchen, then nodded toward the hallway.

"So... Ashley's car still out front."

Morgan didn't say anything.

Jimmy leaned back against the counter, grinning. "Tell me things!"

Morgan tried to suppress a smile but failed. "You're an idiot."

He raised both hands. "Hey, I'm happy for you. I've been waiting on you to make that move since high school."

She didn't respond right away, just gave a small shrug and looked down at the counter. "It's... really good."

Jimmy nodded. "Really good's hard to find. She was worth the wait."

Morgan smiled faintly.

The wind pushed hard against the house, making the porch boards creak. The morning light had shifted to a metallic silver that swallowed the trees.

Ashley stepped into the kitchen a few minutes later, wearing one of Morgan's shirts and still half asleep. "Smells like coffee," she said.

Jimmy grinned. "Morning, sunshine."

She rubbed her eyes and smiled back. "Morning, trouble."

The three of them moved around the kitchen in easy rhythm — eggs in the pan, butter on toast — the kind of quiet preparation that had no real urgency but made an uneasy day feel more normal.

By midday, the wind was steady and loud, shaking the tops of the trees. The air itself had changed — electric, restless, heavy. The marsh beyond the porch rippled in long, uneven waves.

They spent the afternoon securing what they could — sandbags at the doors, tape on the windows, flashlights checked and ready. Jimmy worked without commentary, the practical calm of someone who'd done this year after year.

When the first heavy bands of rain arrived, they gathered in the living room. The light was thin and watery, slipping through the blinds in stripes. Ashley lit a candle on the coffee table.

Outside, the world turned gray.

The hours stretched. The wind built. The radio droned on with coordinates and warnings, then sputtered into static.

By nightfall, the power blinked once, twice, and died

The refrigerator clicked silent. The hum of the house stopped cold.

For a long moment, there was only the sound of the wind — relentless, pressing against the walls. The storm had found them. Even the marsh seemed to breathe differently — water against water, the reeds bowing low in unison.

Rain battered the windows in sheets, and the wind roared down the chimney — a deep, guttural howl that sent a scatter of ash across the hearth. The sound filled the room like breath through an old instrument.

Jimmy and Morgan pushed the coffee table back against the wall. Ashley gathered candles, lighting them one by one. Their flames flickered wildly, bowing to each gust that rattled the glass. They all sat against the old green couch in the middle of the Bar. The spot with the most support possible.

Just after midnight, above the noise — just barely audible — something changed.

At first, it was only a vibration. A hum that didn't belong to the storm.

It seemed to rise from the floorboards, faint but certain, threading through the wind's fury.

Ashley stilled. "Do you hear that?"

Morgan nodded slowly. "Yeah..."

The hum deepened, shaping itself into notes — impossibly soft, impossibly clear.

A man's voice — gentle, distant — began to sing.

"I'll light the fire... you place the flowers... in the vase... that you bought today..."

Ashley's eyes darted toward the console, but the lid was closed and there was no power.

"Morgan," she whispered, "it's not—"

"I know," Morgan said quietly.

The wind howled, battering the porch. Somewhere outside, the old oak groaned — a long, low warning that vibrated through the floor.

The music didn't stop.

"Our house... is a very, very, very fine house..."

The tree's groan deepened into a crack — a splintering, earth-deep sound.

All three instinctively knew to lower their heads and be still.

The impact was deafening — wood splitting, glass shattering, the whole house shaking on its foundation.

Then silence.

The rain still drove against the roof, but inside The Bar, everything held.

Dust drifted through the candlelight like pale smoke. The air smelled of wet pine, of soil torn open. Morgan could taste metal on her tongue — the residue of adrenaline and fear.

She reached out blindly until her hand found Ashley's shoulder.

"Everybody okay?"

Ashley nodded, breath unsteady. "I'm ok.. Are ya'll?"

"Still here," Morgan whispered.

Jimmy stood up. " I'll check the side wall and see what damage was done."

They sat for a moment, just listening — to their own breathing, to the distant rush of water against the porch steps. The storm raged on, but inside, a pocket of calm had formed, a fragile heartbeat of stillness.

And through it all, the music played on — not from the console, not from any speaker, but from the walls themselves.

"Life used to be so hard... now everything is easy... 'cause of you..."

Morgan's voice was a whisper. "It's the cabin."

Ashley's hand found hers.

The wind roared again down the chimney, but this time its voice softened — less fury, more release. The Bar exhaled.

Dust drifted in lazy spirals above the fire grate, catching the glow of the candles as if the house were breathing light back into itself.

Morgan swallowed hard. "Thank you," she said — not sure if she meant it for the house, or for whoever still lingered here.

Outside, the storm tore at the trees, but the structure held. The roof moaned; the windows flexed and shuddered, yet none gave way.

And in that strange, golden quiet — surrounded by chaos, held inside something ancient and alive — The Bar sang.

Their house.

Still standing.

A very, very, very fine house.

CHAPTER 31

The Sun Also Rises

The worst of the storm had moved on by dawn.

What was left of it dragged its gray tail across the marsh — a slow, misting rain that blurred the tree line and left the air heavy and still. The wind had gone quiet except for the occasional restless gust, like a sigh after a long argument.

Morgan stood barefoot on the porch watching the fog shift over the water. The yard was half-flooded, streaked with pine needles and bits of shingle. A plastic lawn chair floated upside down near the edge of the porch, bumping softly against a piling. Everything smelled of rain, brine, and ash — the familiar scent of morning after weather that you knew if you came from this place.

Inside, the low scrape of Jimmy's boots moved from room to room. He'd been up since first light, checking the damage with a flashlight, muttering measurements to himself, occasionally calling out a word or two that didn't bear repeating.

Ashley was still inside, folding blankets, setting things back where they belonged, her movements slow and methodical. She hadn't said much yet. None of them had.

Jimmy appeared in the doorway, one shoulder braced against the frame, his hair damp and sticking up in odd directions.

"Well," he said, "there's good news and bad news."

Morgan didn't turn from the porch rail. "Yeah?"

"Good news is you don't have to worry about that closet door popping open all the time."

He paused, waiting for it to land.

"Bad news…" He tilted his head toward the hall. "Dcor's gone."

Morgan blinked once, then let out a tired laugh — half relief, half disbelief. "Guess it's time to clean out the closet."

Jimmy grinned. "Tree hit square on the side wall. The closet and hallway took most of it. Rest of the house held up fine. I put a couple of tarps up and on the floor so the rain doesn't keep pouring in on the wood. We got lucky."

Morgan nodded, "I'll take lucky. Thank you for staying, Jim."

Jimmy stepped out onto the porch beside Morgan, and put an arm around her shoulder. "You know," he said, "if I didn't know better, I'd swear this old place was built to last forever and knows how to look after itself."

Morgan gave him a sidelong look. "I think it does."

They stood in silence for a few moments, listening to the steady drip of rain off the porch roof. Somewhere in the distance, a frog croaked, brave enough to start singing again already.

Ashley appeared in the doorway, wrapping her arms around herself. She was pale, tired, her hair still damp at the ends. "Just texted my mom. All is fine at their house and in town. Just messy."

"I need to call and check on Margaret. Take a look at that tree."

Jimmy nodded toward the hallway. "Come see."

They followed him through the living room, stepping over damp towels and a scatter of plaster dust from the ceiling. The air grew cooler as they moved down the narrow hall, a faint draft seeping through the cracks where the boards had splintered.

In the middle of the hall, where the closet door used to hang crookedly, there was now only ruin.

The oak had hit almost dead-on — its trunk resting like a fallen monument against the side of the house. The wall bowed inward, splintered but still standing.

Broken sheetrock and a mess of insulation littered the floor. The closet door lay twisted against the opposite wall, its hinges ripped clean away.

Through the jagged hole, Morgan could see daylight — pale and shimmering, like a wound that hadn't stopped bleeding.

Jimmy crouched, poking at the debris with the end of a broom handle. "Looks worse than it is," he said, though his tone suggested otherwise. "Tree caught the edge of the roofline, took part of the siding with it, but the frame held. We can patch it. The main thing's gonna be getting that tree off the side without tearing the rest of it down."

Ashley's voice was soft. "Can we even stay here?"

Jimmy stood, brushing his hands off. "You're fine for now. Structurally it's solid — I checked the beams. But the place will need some real work once it dries out."

Morgan ran her hand along the broken edge of the wall The wood felt damp, soft in places. The faint smell of earth rose from the gap, mixed with the wet, sharp scent of pine sap. She followed the crack upward, her eyes catching on something half-buried under a mound of insulation — a sliver of old newspaper, a rusted nail, and the faint gleam of a hinge.

She knelt, but Jimmy stopped her with a quiet shake of his head. "Not now," he said gently. "Let's get the wall sealed first. Rain's gonna start again before noon."

Morgan nodded. She hadn't been looking forward to cleaning that closet out before and now it was full of WET junk.

They worked for the next few hours without saying much. Jimmy cut a tarp and hammered a temporary frame across the break, sealing out the worst of the damp air. Ashley gathered the fallen clothes from the closet floor — old jackets, a pair of boots, a bent fishing pole — and laid them out to dry on the hearth.

By the time the rain returned, light and steady, the house looked less like a wreck and more like itself again — wounded but standing.

Morgan found herself back on the porch, watching the water recede slowly from the yard before the tide rose again. Ashley joined her, a blanket around her shoulders, two mugs in hand. She handed one to Morgan without speaking.

They stood side by side, sipping coffee gone lukewarm, watching a pair of egrets pick their way across the flooded grass.

"You okay?" Ashley asked. Taking Morgan's hand.

"Yeah," Morgan said, after a moment. "I think so. How are you?"

"I'm okay... glad it wasn't worse than it was and glad we were together."

Morgan smiled and kissed the hand she was holding. "Me too."

After a while, Jimmy joined them, lowering himself into the chair opposite theirs. He looked like he'd aged a few years overnight, his face lined with exhaustion and rain. "Got a message out to a guy in town about the tree. He's backed up but said he'll get to us by tomorrow if he can."

Morgan nodded. "Thank you."

He shrugged. "Not my first rodeo." He leaned forward, elbows on his knees. "I'll stay the night again, if that's alright. I don't like leaving y'all alone with the wall still open just in case that tree shifts."

Ashley nodded quickly. "Please do."

The wind picked up again — not hard, but insistent. It moved through the trees in long, low waves. Morgan found herself glancing toward the hallway again, where the tarp rippled faintly in the draft.

"Feels different in here now," Jimmy said quietly.

Ashley looked over. "How so?"

He thought for a moment. "Like something finally settled. Almost... lighter."

Morgan didn't answer, but she understood what he meant. The Bar had always carried a certain weight — not sadness, exactly, but something unspoken, hanging in the walls. Now, even with the damage, the air felt hopeful somehow.

Jimmy stood and stretched. "I'm gonna head out, grab my truck before it sinks any deeper in that mud and see how bad it is on the way to town. Be back after lunch."

He started down the steps, his boots sinking into the wet ground.

When he was gone, the quiet folded back over them.

Ashley leaned against Morgan's shoulder "It really does feel lighter," she said.

Morgan turned her head slightly. "Yeah. It does."

The rain thickened again — soft, rhythmic, almost musical. For a moment, it sounded like the faint hum that had risen through the floor the night before.

Ashley's hand found Morgan's, fingers lacing easily. "Do you think... that was him?"

Morgan hesitated. "I don't know but it felt like someone was taking care of us."

Ashley nodded. "It did."

They stayed like that, quiet, watching the day unfold — the storm now just a memory unraveling itself across the horizon.

By midafternoon, the worst of the water had drained away. The yard looked bruised but intact. A few shingles lay scattered in the grass, and one of the porch steps had come loose from its frame. Morgan made a mental note to fix it, the thought landing with the odd comfort of normalcy.

Inside, she swept the floor, shook out the rugs, and tried to coax the house back into order. Ashley worked beside her, humming softly — an old song Morgan recognized but couldn't place.

As the day faded, the light grew golden again, slanting through the streaked windows in long, uneven bands. Dust hung in the air, catching the light like motes of fire. The Bar didn't feel broken. It felt alive — changed, but steady.

When Jimmy returned, he brought sandwiches, bottled water, and a small generator he'd borrowed from a friend. They ate by candlelight again, laughing in fits over nothing, the way people do when they've been through something together and returned to normalcy on the other side.

After dinner, they sat in the living room — the same green couch, the same soft shadows — and listened to the sound of crickets weaving their way back into the night. The news showed footage of the damage that had been done in the Low Country and they were all glad that it wasn't worse.

"We'll start clearing the tree tomorrow," Jimmy said. "You'll be able to see what's left of the wall once we get that trunk off."

Morgan nodded. "I'll help."

"You'll supervise," he said, smirking. "You've done enough damage for one storm."

She kicked at his boot lightly and grinned back.

It was near midnight when the generator sputtered off. The house went quiet again, but this time the darkness didn't feel heavy.

Morgan lay awake, listening to the wind move gently around the corners of the Bar. Every creak, every sigh of the house felt familiar now — not ominous, but alive.

Beside her, Ashley stirred. "You awake?"

"Yeah."

Ashley shifted closer and put her arm around Morgan. "I keep thinking about that sound. The music."

"I know," Morgan whispered. "Me too."

Ashley hesitated. "I don't know what it could have been. All I can think of is your granddad."

Morgan thought for a long moment before answering. "Maybe he wanted us to know the house was going to hold."

Ashley turned over and Morgan lay near her... holding her.

When sleep finally came, it was deep and dreamless.

Outside, the moon broke through the clouds for the first time in days, laying a soft silver light across the marsh, the porch, and the battered side of the house where the oak had struck.

Inside the hall, behind the tarp and the broken boards, something small and square sat buried beneath the debris — dry, untouched, waiting.

CHAPTER 32

The light of the world

By morning, the world had gone still again.

The storm had carried itself off toward the Atlantic, leaving behind a quiet only broken by the sound of far-off chainsaws. The marsh was flat and silver, its edges softened by fog. Puddles mirrored the bluish sky, broken only by the ripples of a wind too tired to keep blowing.

Morgan stood on the porch steps with a mug of coffee, her bare feet on damp wood. The yard looked different — stripped, scoured. The great oak lay splayed against the side of the house like a fallen monument. Its leaves were dull, its limbs tangled with shingle and siding. The smell of wood and wet earth hung thick in the air.

Inside, Jimmy moved from room to room, taking measurements and speaking to someone on the phone about tools needed.

Ashley was at the table, hair tied up, hands wrapped around her mug, checking her email and texts.

"I'm going to need to head to the store. The guys are swamped and supplies are going fast. You good here? Need me to bring you anything later?" she asked.

Morgan smiled faintly. "You'll be swamped. All I need is you, beautiful person."

"Awww," Ashley said, standing to kiss her on the cheek. "So sweet … maybe me and a burger if I can find one?"

Morgan caught her hand as she turned to leave. "Be careful, please … and yes to the burger."

Ashley smiled.

By the time Ashley's truck disappeared down the road, Jimmy's friends had arrived — two men in their forties, quiet and efficient, the kind who didn't talk unless there was a reason. They looked once at the fallen oak, then set to work.

The sound of chainsaws broke through the still air — metal teeth biting through wet wood and sawdust flying in pale sprays. It wasn't chaos, though. It was rhythm. It was work. The kind of work that meant things were going back to normal.

Well, normal for The Bar.

Morgan stayed on the porch, watching. The sound was oddly comforting, a steady counterpoint to the storm's memory. Every few minutes, Jimmy called for a cut or a pull, his voice calm and sure. The house seemed to settle with every section removed, like it was exhaling.

A little before noon, Margaret's sedan appeared at the edge of the drive, tires cutting slow through the mud. She parked beside the trucks and got out carefully, her white sneakers already spattered brown.

"Well, Lord," she said, looking up at the roofline. "I almost had a heart attack when I turned the corner and saw that tree!"

Morgan smiled and hugged her. "You should've heard it hit."

"I'm surprised I didn't hear it from my house," Margaret said, stepping back to look at her niece. "You look better than I expected."

"I feel better than I should with no sleep."

Margaret looked toward the men at work. "You got a good crew."

"Jimmy called in a few favors."

She smiled knowingly. "That boy would do anything for you."

Jimmy appeared from around the corner of the house, pulling his gloves off. "We'll have it clear by mid-afternoon," he said. "Just gotta be careful with the base near the wall."

Margaret nodded. "You're a good man, Jimmy."

He shrugged. "I try."

As they talked, one of the men waved him over. Jimmy jogged off, but not before leaning closer to Margaret and lowering his voice. "You know," he said with a grin, "your girl's finally got herself someone good."

Margaret raised a brow. "That so?"

He nodded toward the road where Ashley's truck had gone. "You can see it on her face."

Margaret smiled — a small, quiet thing. "Well, it's about time somebody made her smile again."

The chainsaws wound down by late afternoon. What was left of the tree lay stacked in neat, round sections beside the fence. The men packed their tools, and Jimmy began boarding the wall with plywood. The house looked wounded but intact — its scars clean and honest.

Margaret stood beside Morgan on the porch. The light had gone warm and gold again, spilling across the wet yard.

"She'll be all right," Margaret said, meaning the cabin, though maybe not only the cabin.

Morgan nodded. "Feels like she already is."

"You don't have to tell me anything, honey," Margaret said after a pause. "I just want you to know … I see it. I'm glad you both have each other."

Morgan looked over, startled, but Margaret was still looking at the yard.

"Jimmy's got a big mouth," Morgan said softly.

Margaret smiled. "He's got a kind heart. And I've got eyes." She reached out, squeezed Morgan's hand. "You look happy. That's all I need to know."

Ashley didn't make it home until early evening.

Her truck headlights cut through the dark, bouncing across puddles as she pulled up the drive. Inside, the house smelled faintly of sawdust and rain. The plywood along the hallway gleamed pale against the darker paneling.

"Looks good," she said, stepping into the kitchen, exhaustion written across her face. "How bad was it?"

"Not that bad," Morgan said. "We cleaned up most of the mess. Jimmy patched the frame. Just need a real fix when things settle."

Ashley poured herself a glass of water, leaning against the counter. "I must've sold every piece of plywood and roll of duct tape in the county today."

"I missed you," said Morgan with a funny pout, giving Ashley a warm hug.

Margaret came out of the hallway, wiping her hands on a towel. "We were just about to start clearing what's left in the closet."

"I can help," Ashley said.

"Are you sure?" asked Margaret. "You've been working all day, honey."

"Definitely ... I found a second wind." Ashley smiled and winked at Morgan.

The three of them stood in the hall a few minutes later. The air still smelled faintly of damp wood. Sunlight leaked through a thin crack at the top of the plywood panel, cutting a slanted beam across the floor.

Most of the debris had already been pushed aside — splintered boards, torn insulation, bits of fabric. What was left was a narrow pile against the inside wall, dark with dust.

Margaret handed Morgan a pair of gloves. "Last of it," she said. "Then we'll call it done."

They worked quietly.

Margaret sorted what could be saved — an old lantern, a fishing pole missing its reel. Ashley swept the smaller bits into a box. Morgan knelt, tugging free the base of a collapsed shelf. It came loose with a soft sigh, dragging something else with it — a small box of extremely old Christmas ornaments that might still shine again come December.

"I don't see anything else back there. Can I hold the flashlight?" asked Morgan, already reaching for it.

"You may have to walk back in there. This closet is deep, hon," said Margaret.

Morgan made her way to the very back to check against the left wall, which was still mostly intact. There was a box there that had been overlooked, wedged tight where the boards had buckled.

"Ash, can you help me get this one unstuck?"

Ashley followed the beam of light, crouched beside her, and helped pull the box free. Together they set it down on the floor between them.

"I have no idea what that could be," said Margaret. The box was wrapped in plain brown paper — apparently for decades, judging by the dust that coated it.

They carried it to the living room, brushing away years of grime and bits of bark that had fallen from the tree.

Morgan ran her hand across the top. "Well," she said quietly, "that's been sitting a while."

The paper tore with a dry whisper, releasing a faint smell of dust and time.

Beneath the brown paper was bright pink birthday wrapping covered with balloons. There was also a small tag attached with an ancient piece of tape.

Happy Double Digits, sweetheart! Love Granddad.

For a moment, no one moved.

They stared at the gift as if they were seeing a ghost.

Finally, Margaret found her voice. "This was your surprise," she said softly. "He must've hidden it in the back so no one would find it until he could bring it out. It's the only place nobody would have looked."

CHAPTER 33

A *gift of true things*

The house was still.

Not silent, exactly — the kind of stillness that followed a long cry. The kind that held the air tenderly, as if the walls themselves were holding you up.

Morgan sat on the floor beside the coffee table with the box in front of her. Ashley sat close enough so Morgan could feel her near, and Margaret was in Granddad's old chair, her hands folded loosely in her lap.

The weight of the moment pressed quietly against the room — not heavy, but certain.

Margaret finally exhaled and said softly, "Well, honey, I think you should open it. Do you want to be alone?"

"No. Stay." Morgan looked down at the box. The birthday paper was still bright under the layer of brown — pink balloons, little cartoon presents, a pattern that belonged to another decade. The old tape was brittle, the corners curling with time. She brushed her thumb across the tag.

Happy Double Digits, sweetheart. Love, Granddad.

She smiled faintly, but her chest ached. "I can't believe this has been sitting here all this time."

Margaret nodded. "He had it hidden good. I don't think any of us ever cleaned that closet properly. We were too scared it'd all fall in on us."

Morgan slid her fingers beneath the paper and began to pull. It tore softly, the sound dry as autumn leaves. Beneath it was a layer of thin cardboard, yellowed with age. She loosened the flaps and peeled them back.

Inside sat a small green case. The leather was cracked along the edges but still held its shape very well. The metal latch wasn't tarnished, the handle wasn't dull. The double wrapping had done its unintended job.

Morgan hesitated, then looked up at Margaret. "Do you remember him ever having something like this?"

Margaret leaned forward, eyes narrowing. "I have never seen it before, honey."

Morgan ran her hand along the top of the case. The surface was cool, the color soft like old glass. She lifted the latch. It stuck for a moment before giving way with a sharp metallic click.

When she opened it, the air changed.

The faint smell of oil and old paper rose like a memory — not unpleasant, but grounding. The kind of smell you only notice in things that were loved. Inside a Royal Quiet DeLuxe in sea-green enamel. The keys were round and clean, the letters set in crisp white.

On top of it, resting neatly against the platen, was a single envelope.

Morgan reached for it, but her hands trembled.

Margaret nodded toward it.

The envelope was sealed. Across the front, in her grandfather's careful, slanted hand, was written:

For Morgan – On your 10th birthday

Her throat tightened. She eased a finger under the flap and lifted it open. Inside was one sheet of lined paper, folded twice. The ink was faded blue, the handwriting steady.

Morgan read aloud:

"Happy Happy Birthday!! Ten years old. Double digits! That's a fine age to start thinking big, and I've got a feeling you're already doing just that.

This here is a Royal portable typewriter. Supposedly belonged to a man I admire a great deal —

Ernest Hemingway. You don't know this, but I saw his home in Cuba a long time ago when I was a young man. The caretaker swore it was his. Maybe so. Either way, it's a special tool — same as a hammer or a wrench — but with stories in it.

I love the way you sit at the kitchen table and make up stories for the family, whole worlds built out of air. You tell them like you'd been there yourself. That's a gift, Morgan. Don't let it go quiet. When you write, don't worry about getting it right — just get it true to you. Big words don't make it better. Big feelings do. So write BIG. Write honest. Write about the things that scare you, and the things that make you laugh. The rest will take care of itself. I'm so proud of you. I hope you know just how much. You've got something special, and I can't wait to see where it takes you in life. I'm your biggest fan!

Happy Birthday, baby.

Love, Your Granddad"

When her voice broke, Ashley reached over and touched her leg, grounding her.

Margaret's eyes glistened.

Morgan looked down at the letter again. "He wasn't planning on not giving it to me himself," she said softly.

The words hung in the air like a breath that wouldn't leave.

Margaret wiped her eyes.

Ashley sat closer, her hand still on Morgan's knee. "He loved you so much."

Morgan nodded, but tears kept coming — slow, quiet, steady. Not the kind she'd ever let herself cry before. Not the kind that hurt.

"He didn't leave on purpose," she said, voice low.

"I know," Margaret said, crying freely now. She knelt to the floor and pulled her close.

The house seemed to listen with them. The wind outside softened, moving through the trees in long, even breaths. Somewhere in the marsh, a heron cried — a thin, lonely sound that faded into stillness.

When Morgan finally lifted her head, her eyes were red but calm. The letter trembled slightly in her hand.

They sat together for a long time after that — the three of them. The candlelight flickered across their faces, across the green enamel of the typewriter, across the edges of the letter that had waited so long to be read.

Eventually, Margaret stood and went to the kitchen for a glass of water.

Morgan studied the beautiful gift. She could tell that it had been cared for. It smelled freshly overhauled. The ribbons were brand new.

Morgan turned the typewriter toward her. She pressed a key. It moved smoothly, as if it had never rested.

Click.

As she removed it from the case, two other pieces of paper lay underneath. One was a handwritten receipt from December 1994. It showed the typewriter had been shipped from Florida. The other was an older piece of paper, folded like it had once been in an envelope.

Ashley reached for her hand. "You okay?"

Morgan took a long breath, eyes on the letter. "I think so. It's like... everything that was stuck just came loose."

Ashley hugged her and held her.

Morgan opened the final piece of paper and noticed it was stationery. At the top, in a very old printed font:

From the desk of Ernest Hemingway

Finca Vigía, San Francisco de Paula, Cuba

It was handwritten with ink that had faded to brown over time. The date was June 4, 1954, and it was addressed to Mr. Billy Langford.

Your story is good. Keep writing.

You're doin' just fine, kid.

A faint curl of smoke drifted through the air — sweet, old, and gone before she could place it.

You're doin' just fine, kid.

She remembered that night on the couch after drinking too much. The breath on her ear. Those exact words.

As night deepened, Ashley helped Margaret load some of the things from the closet into the back of her car Morgan stayed behind, staring at the typewriter. The green casing caught the lamplight like glass from the riverbed. She reached forward and brushed a bit of dust from the Royal emblem.

Then she set it on the table by the window — the one she'd been using to half-heartedly write for weeks.

She sat. The chair creaked under her weight. The air smelled of rain and metal and faint candle wax.

Her fingers hovered over the keys, hesitant but sure.

She fed a sheet of lined paper through the roller, turned the knob, and lined it up. The carriage dinged softly, a sound that seemed to echo through the whole house.

For a long moment, she didn't move. Then she began to type.

The house stood through the storm. We did too.

There's something still here — in the walls, in the air. I think I finally understand what he meant by writing true.

I think maybe that's what he was trying to do all along. Maybe they both were.

She stopped, sat back, and smiled. The sound of the keys had settled into her chest like a heartbeat.

Ashley came up behind her quietly and rested a hand on her shoulder. "First page?"

Morgan nodded. "Yeah."

Ashley leaned down and kissed the top of her head. "It's a good one."

Margaret stood in the doorway, watching them, her smile quiet and full. "He'd be proud," she said. "Both of you."

The room felt alive — warm, breathing, whole.

Outside, the tide rose again, lapping gently at the pilings. The night was clear, stars trembling faintly above the marsh.

Morgan looked out through the window, past the reflection of the lamp, to where the water met the horizon.

For the first time in a long time, she didn't feel haunted.

She felt whole.

She turned back to the typewriter and placed her fingers on the keys again.

Click. Click. Click.

The sound was soft, steady — like rain against the roof.

CHAPTER 34

We're doin' fine

By late morning, the house had settled again.

The air smelled of wood dust and coffee, faintly sweet from the bakery box Margaret had brought that morning. The plywood over the hallway still caught the light in a strange way — a pale scar against the darker walls — but even that was starting to feel like part of the house now.

Morgan sat at the kitchen table with Ashley, both of them wrapped in the quiet that comes after hard days. Outside, Jimmy and Pete were clearing the last of the tree trunk, stacking the rounds neatly beside the shed.

It sounded like order returning — chainsaws winding down, shovels hitting damp earth, the low rhythm of people making things right again.

Margaret had been gone since early morning, saying only that she had "some errands to run."

When her sedan pulled back into the drive, it kicked up a spray of mud. She stepped out carrying a thin manila envelope and the look of someone who had carried the weight of a long morning but was finally ready to set it down.

Morgan met her at the porch steps. "You okay?"

Margaret smiled, tired but sure. "I am now."

She came inside and set the envelope on the table between them, smoothing it once with her hand.

"It's done," she said quietly. "I went down to the coroner's office first thing."

Ashley turned from the counter. "Already?"

Margaret nodded. "I showed him everything — the note about Knowles, the gift wrapping, the birthday tag. I told him about the tape, too — the date, the things your granddad said that morning before he left. He didn't argue. Said sometimes they get it wrong the first time because the pieces aren't all there."

Morgan stared at the envelope. "And?"

Margaret tapped it gently. "And it's official now. The cause of death has been amended to accidental. He said it should've read that way all along."

The words hung there a moment before settling.

Ashley reached for Morgan's hand under the table.

Margaret pulled out the paper — crisp, newly printed, the county seal faint at the top. She slid it toward her niece.

Morgan read the line once, twice, letting it sink in. The words blurred as her eyes filled, but she smiled through it.

"He didn't leave on purpose," she said softly.

Margaret shook her head. "No, sweetheart. He didn't."

Morgan exhaled, a long, trembling breath that seemed to empty years of quiet ache.

Margaret laid her hand over hers. "He wanted you to know that all along. He just couldn't stay long enough to tell you himself."

Ashley brushed a tear from her cheek. "You did it, Margaret."

"I just took the paper where it needed to go," she said. "He did the rest."

They sat like that for a while — no speeches, no ceremony, just the low hum of the refrigerator and the steady tick of the clock. The house seemed to breathe with them, a long exhale through its old bones.

Jimmy came in a few minutes later, wiping his hands on a rag. "Tree's gone," he said. "Yard looks halfway decent again."

Margaret turned toward him with a small smile. "Good. Because we've got news."

He caught the tone before the words. "They changed it?"

She nodded. "Accident. It's right now."

Jimmy let out a quiet whistle and set the rag on the counter. "Thank goodness." He looked at Morgan, his expression softening. "Feels like something's settled, doesn't it?"

"It does," Morgan said. "More than I can explain."

That afternoon, the sky cleared to a bright, forgiving blue. The air felt washed clean, like the kind of day you couldn't waste even if you tried.

Jimmy packed up his tools but promised to be back in the morning to start planning the rebuild. Margaret stayed behind, helping Ashley put the kitchen back together.

Morgan stood at the edge of the porch watching the light stretch long across the marsh. Everything shimmered — the puddles in the yard, the water beyond, even the boards of the porch, still damp but catching the sun like old glass.

Margaret stepped out beside her. "Feels different out here now," she said.

Morgan nodded. "Yeah. Everything feels different."

"That's how truth works," Margaret said. "Doesn't fix the loss, but it takes the weight off."

She reached over and tucked a loose strand of hair behind Morgan's ear — a gesture she'd done a thousand times before when Morgan was small and unsure of the world.

They stayed like that a long while, side by side in the soft, humming quiet. Inside, the typewriter sat in its new place by the window, a green glint of possibility waiting for the next page.

When Margaret finally left, she kissed Morgan's cheek and said, "He'd be proud of you, you know."

"I hope so."

"Oh, I know so," Margaret said, smiling as she stepped off the porch. "And so am I."

That night, after the house settled and Ashley turned off the last lamp, Morgan stood by the writing table. The moon poured through the window, silver and slow. Ashley was already asleep, her breathing slow and steady.

Morgan ran her fingers over the smooth enamel of the Royal, tracing the edge of the "R" like she was learning it for the first time.

It felt like both an ending and a beginning — not a chapter closing, but a door finally opening.

Morgan never actually knew who was sharing the Bar with her those first few months. Papa? Granddad? Maybe both or just the Bar itself.

She sat down, rolled a clean page into the platen, and just looked at it. The keys waited patiently, like an old friend.

In the silence, she could almost hear his voice again — steady, gentle, amused.

You're doin' just fine, kid.

She smiled through the ache. "I know," she whispered. "We are."

CHAPTER 35

The Last Good Seat at the Bar

Morgan's day began soft and clear, with the faint smell of salt riding the breeze.

Two weeks had passed since Margaret's visit to the coroner, and The Bar was beginning to feel whole again. The new boards along the hallway gleamed pale and unpainted, the scent of cut wood still sharp in the air. A carpenter would come soon to finish Morgan's new writing room, but for now, the space stood open — a blank page waiting to be filled.

Morgan sat at her makeshift desk with her coffee cooling beside the green Royal — an old card table she'd pulled from the utility room. Sunlight slipped through the blinds, striping the table in gold. The house creaked and sighed as it always had, but the sound was no longer lonely. It was the sound of a place breathing deeply again.

Her phone buzzed on the counter.

Claire.

She smiled as she answered.

"Hey, stranger."

"Hey yourself," Claire said. "I was starting to think you'd gone off-grid entirely."

Morgan laughed. "Pretty close. You holding up?"

"Oh, you know. Atlanta's still Atlanta. Your plants are thriving, by the way. I think they like me better."

"I believe it."

There was a pause, warm and familiar. Claire had been with her through every deadline, every bad draft, every hangover that followed the kind of night she didn't want to remember. It felt right to tell her first.

"Listen," Morgan said. "I'm going to stay. Here, I mean. For good."

"I kind of figured." Claire's voice softened. "You sound different. You sound calm."

"Yeah," Morgan said. "That's exactly what it feels like. I've reached out to a few old friends who are gonna send some work my way."

"I'm proud of you," Claire said. "You did the brave thing."

Morgan smiled into the phone. "Thanks for holding on to everything while I figured this out."

"Anytime. And if you ever change your mind, the spare key's where it's always been."

"I won't," Morgan said. "But it's nice to know."

Claire made plans to come visit soon, and when the call ended, the silence that followed wasn't empty. It was steady.

By late morning, Jimmy's truck rumbled up the drive.

He climbed out with a grin and a grease-smudged ball cap.

"Morning, ladies!" Jimmy called through the screen. "I need to borrow something."

Ashley poked her head out of the writing room, where she'd been sanding the trim. "That's usually how it starts."

Jimmy laughed. "I'm doing a pig pickin' this weekend and I need to borrow the big stock pot — the good one."

Morgan grinned. "Granddad's barbecue sauce?"

"Oh yeah," Jimmy said. "None better."

Morgan reached above the refrigerator and quietly pulled down a half-empty bottle of bourbon. "You'll need this, too."

Jimmy took it, raising it like a toast. "The good stuff. You sure?"

"I don't need it," Morgan said quietly. "But I know that sauce does."

Jimmy studied her face for a moment, then nodded. "Okay... everybody's coming for dinner tomorrow afternoon. Ash's folks, too. I already stopped by the hardware store."

"Sounds great, cousin."

He gave her a quick hug, the kind that didn't need words, and carried the pot and bottle out to the truck. The sound of his laughter drifted back through the open door, blending with the hum of the cicadas.

Later that afternoon, the sky was cloudless, the air full of the green scent of pine and the distant murmur of the river. Ashley came home early from the store, her hair pulled back, shoulders misted with sawdust.

"How'd it go?" Morgan asked from the porch, where she sat with her notebook open but empty.

"Busy. Everybody in town's fixing something. Feels good, though. To be busy."

Morgan nodded. "Yeah. It does."

Ashley dropped into the chair beside her, kicked off her shoes, and looked out toward the marsh. "They're almost done inside. I was thinking... we leave that writing room simple. Just a desk, a shelf, and maybe one chair."

Morgan smiled. "That's all it needs."

"Paint or stain?"

"Neither. I like it natural."

Ashley reached over and took her hand. "You look like you belong here."

Morgan turned her head, meeting her eyes. "So do you."

They stayed like that a while, watching the light shift across the yard — the egrets tracing slow arcs over the water, the tide beginning its lazy return. Somewhere down the dirt road, Jimmy's radio played faintly through the open windows of his truck, an old song that sounded like every summer they'd ever spent.

That night, after dinner, they left the dishes in the sink and sat by the open window. The moon was nearly full casting a soft wash of silver across the porch. The Bar smelled of fresh wood and lemon oil.

Morgan rested her head on Ashley's shoulder. "Do you ever think about how different life has turned out?"

Ashley nodded. "Every day. But I think it turned out the way it was supposed to."

They didn't say anything else for a long time. The house was quiet except for the slow ticking of the kitchen clock and the rustle of night wind through the palmettos.

When they finally went to bed, the windows were open and the air was cool. The typewriter sat by the window — green enamel catching the moonlight like river glass. The next morning came gray and a bit wind-stirred.

Ashley was up before sunrise, dressed for work, tying her hair back as Morgan poured the first cup of coffee. The floorboards creaked the same way they always had. It was their music now.

Ashley leaned down and kissed her, slow and sure. "Write big. See you this afternoon."

Morgan looked up, smiling. "I love you."

"I know," Ashley said. "I love you too."

She grabbed her keys and stepped out onto the porch. The screen door whispered shut behind her. A moment later, Morgan heard the engine start, the tires crunch down the dirt drive, then fade into the quiet.

The house settled.

Morgan turned back to the table. The typewriter waited, a blank page rolled into the platen. Outside, the wind pushed softly against the screens, the marsh whispering its low, steady rhythm.

Morgan pulled a few albums from the collection and placed them on the changer. The first album dropped onto the platter. The needle landed. Van Morrison "Into The Mystic."

"We were born before the wind. Also younger than the sun."

She sat down, set her coffee beside her, and rested her fingers on the keys. The air held that same stillness as before — not silence, but peace.

Then she began the story the only way she knew how — from the beginning.

CHAPTER 1

I sat on the edge of the couch, elbows on my knees, staring into the quiet.

Thank you for spending time at The Bar!

If this story meant something to you, I would be grateful if you left a short review on the website where you purchased the book.

Your words help other readers find their way here, too.

All The Bright Precious Things

A Novel

Coming next from Trade Street Press.

www.tradestreetpress.com

Acknowledgments:

To Gina Heron with Creative Agility, LLC for her thoughtful editorial insight and encouragement.

Check out her work on Instagram! @ginaherontoday

And to my friend Sage. Your advice, proofreading and feedback were invaluable.

Just the Way You Are
Written by Billy Joel
Performed by Billy Joel
© 1977 Impulsive Music (ASCAP)

In a Sentimental Mood
Composed by Duke Ellington
Lyrics by Manny Kurtz and Irving Mills
Performed by Duke Ellington
© 1935 (Renewed) EMI Mills Music Inc. (ASCAP)

Your Cheatin' Heart
Written and Performed by Hank Williams
© 1952 Acuff-Rose Publications, Inc. (ASCAP)

Girl from the North Country
Written and Performed by Bob Dylan
© 1963 Special Rider Music (ASCAP)

Jambalaya (On the Bayou)
Written by Hank Williams
Performed by Hank Williams
© 1952 Acuff-Rose Publications, Inc. (ASCAP)

Be Young, Be Foolish, Be Happy
Written by J.R. Cobb and Ray Whitley
Performed by The Tams
© 1967 Lowery Music Co. Inc. (BMI)

Stardust
Composed by Hoagy Carmichael
Lyrics by Mitchell Parish
Performed by Willie Nelson (from *Stardust*, 1978)
© 1929 EMI Mills Music Inc. (ASCAP) (Renewed)

A Kiss to Build a Dream On
Lyrics by Oscar Hammerstein II & Jack Hammer
Music by Bert Kalmar
Performed by Louis Armstrong
© 1935 Sony/ATV Harmony (ASCAP)

King of the Road
Written and Performed by Roger Miller
© 1964 Tree Publishing Co., Inc. (BMI)

Walkin' After Midnight
Written by Don Hecht and Alan Block
Performed by Patsy Cline
© 1956 Knox Music, Inc. / Ben Block Music, Inc.
(BMI)

Skylark
Music by Hoagy Carmichael
Lyrics by Johnny Mercer
Performed by Ella Fitzgerald
© 1941 Sony/ATV Harmony (ASCAP)

Sawgrass
Written by Emily Coleman
© 2025 Trade Street Press (BMI)

Feels Like Rain
 Written and Performed by John Hiatt
© 1988 Warner-Tamerlane Publishing Corp. / Wixen
Music Publishing (BMI)

Do You Want to Know a Secret
Written by John Lennon and Paul McCartney
Performed by The Beatles
© 1963 Sony/ATV Tunes LLC (BMI)

Cupid
Written and Performed by Sam Cooke
© 1961 ABKCO Music, Inc. (BMI)

Sunday Morning Coming Down
Written by Kris Kristofferson
Performed by Johnny Cash
© 1969 Combine Music Corp. (BMI)

Carolina in My Mind
Written and Performed by James Taylor
© 1968 Country Road Music, Inc. (BMI)

Our House
Written by Graham Nash
Performed by Crosby, Stills, Nash & Young
© 1970 Nash Notes (BMI)

Into the Mystic
Written and Performed by Van Morrison
© 1970 Warner Bros. Music (ASCAP)

All song titles, lyrics, and artist names referenced in this book remain the property of their respective copyright holders.

Lyrics are quoted under fair use for literary and artistic purposes. No claim of ownership is made, and no commercial use of the lyrics is intended.